Alessand[ro]
Tall, dark and mysterious.

The quintessential playboy, or so the rumors went. Hero in disguise or con man with an agenda?

Colleen would give the charming Italian the benefit of the doubt, since Alessandro had protected Holly and Jake when they'd needed it.

But if Alessandro Donato was up to no good, she'd nail his hide to the wall all over the front page of the *Colorado Springs Sentinel,* regardless of how attractive she found him.

* * *

FAITH AT THE CROSSROADS: Can faith and love sustain two families against a diabolical enemy?

Books by Terri Reed

Love Inspired Suspense

Strictly Confidential #21

Love Inspired

Love Comes Home #258
A Sheltering Love #302

TERRI REED

grew up in a small town nestled in the foothills of the Sierra Nevada. To entertain herself, she created stories in her head. And when she put those stories to paper, her teachers in grade school, high school and college encouraged her imagination. Living in Italy as an exchange student whetted her appetite for travel, and modeling in New York, Chicago and San Francisco gave her a love for the big city, as well. She has also coached gymnastics and taught in a preschool. She enjoys walks on the beach, hikes in the mountains and exploring cities. From a young age she attended church, but it wasn't until her thirties that she really understood the meaning of a faith-filled life. Now living in Portland, Oregon, with her college-sweetheart husband, two wonderful children, a rambunctious Australian shepherd and a fat guinea pig, she feels blessed to be able to share her stories and her faith with the world. She loves to hear from readers at P.O. Box 19555, Portland, OR, 97280.

Terri Reed

Strictly Confidential

Steeple
Hill®

Published by Steeple Hill Books™

Special thanks and acknowledgment are given to
Terri Reed for her contribution to the
FAITH AT THE CROSSROADS miniseries.
Thank you to Diane Dietz and Steeple Hill for this
opportunity to work on this series. I had such fun
working with and learning from the other authors.

STEEPLE HILL BOOKS

Steeple
Hill®

ISBN 0-373-87365-4

STRICTLY CONFIDENTIAL

www.SteepleHill.com

Printed in U.S.A.

Draw close to God, and God will draw close to you.
—*James* 4:8

CAST OF CHARACTERS

Alessandro Donato—Tall, dark and handsome, he showed up wherever there was trouble. Was Alessandro working for the European Union, as he claimed, or for the bad guys reviving the drug trade in Colorado Springs?

Colleen Montgomery—Her reporter's nose smelled a story brewing…and Alessandro was her prime target. But would her curiosity get her killed?

Dahlia Sainsbury—The museum curator wanted Colleen out of the picture—because she wanted Alessandro for herself or was there a more devious motive?

ONE

"This is strictly confidential. Off the record. Mum's the word."

Colleen Montgomery paused in the act of pulling out a navy business suit from her closet to arch a brow at her sister-in-law, Holly.

Holly flipped back her long dark-brown hair, which she'd curled and wore loose rather than in her traditional ponytail. "I'm serious. You can't tell anyone what I'm about to tell you."

Grimacing, Colleen stared. "That's like asking me not to breathe."

Holly rolled her brown eyes. "And you're not wearing that suit. You're wearing the dress I brought you."

Rehanging the suit, Colleen gestured with her hands. "Hello. I'm an investigative reporter. My life is about telling everyone what I see and hear."

"Promise me, okay?" Holly shifted on the bed where she'd sat as soon as she'd entered Colleen's bedroom. She was wearing a pretty lilac party dress that flattered her even with her bulging tummy, and she'd come in on the pretext of bringing a dress for Colleen to wear to the museum gala. Now, however, Colleen suspected her sister-in-law had another agenda, one that brought worry to her pretty brown eyes and marred the normally smooth skin between her brunette eyebrows.

"Is this about my brother?" Colleen moved to her vanity to brush her blond hair. "'Cause if it is, I'm not sure I want to hear it."

Holly twisted her diamond wedding ring. "It is about him and me."

Colleen held up a hand and met Holly's gaze through the mirror's reflection. "I can already tell this is going to be more information than I want to hear about my big brother. Unless he's dragged you back into the FBI with him, in which case I'll go clobber him on the head. Considering you're carrying my niece or nephew, the FBI is not a good place for you."

Holly grinned and patted her burgeoning belly. "No, of course not." She lifted the sheath dress off the bed. "Here, put this on while I explain."

Eyeing the little black shift with trepidation, Colleen said, "You really think I should wear that?"

"Yes. For once dress like a woman."

Colleen pulled a face. "Cute."

Holly laughed. "You know what I mean. All you

wear are pants and button-down blouses. Time to move out of your comfort zone."

Colleen took the dress. It wasn't exactly something that could be worn while chasing down a story, not if you still hoped to be taken seriously. Of course, tonight she hardly expected to find anything of interest worth reporting. She moved into the bathroom to dress. "Fine. Start talking."

"Do you remember when Victor Convy kidnapped me?"

Colleen scoffed as she changed out of the jeans and cotton T-shirt she'd put on after showering earlier. "Hard to forget a thing like that."

"Right. Well, something happened that I never told anyone about."

Anticipation of a story fluttered in Colleen's belly. Her parents often joked that she'd greeted the world with a notepad and pen in hand. "Okay."

"Remember how Jake had said he couldn't remember if he'd shot Convy or not because of his concussion?"

Stepping into the dress, Colleen made a noise of affirmation. The fear of losing her brother still gnawed at her like a dog with a bone. But that came with love. She had no choice but to love her brothers and now their wives, but thought thankfully that she didn't have time for a romantic love. She didn't want to carry around that kind of fear.

"He didn't," Holly said.

Colleen's heart picked up speed at the juicy tidbit of information. She stepped out of the bathroom, holding the dress to her chest. "*You* did?"

"No." Holly lowered her voice and a conspiratorial light entered her eyes. "Alessandro Donato did."

"What?!" The dress dropped to the floor and pooled around Colleen's ankles. She quickly pulled it back up and slipped her arms through the holes.

Holly eagerly nodded. "I'm telling you, he came out of the trees dressed all in black like some superhero, shot Convy, and made certain Jake was alive before untying me. Then he disappeared as stealthily as he came when he heard the sirens coming."

Colleen blinked, unsure how to process Holly's tale. "So you're saying that Alessandro Donato rescued you and my brother from Convy?"

Eyes wide, Holly bobbed her head. "That's what I'm saying."

"Wow! That's huge."

Rumor had it that the mysterious newcomer, although Lidia Vance's nephew, had somehow been responsible for the shooting of his uncle, Mayor Maxwell Vance.

How could Donato save one man's life and then be suspected of trying to take the life of someone in his own family?

She'd seen Donato at church with his aunt and

cousins, but was that just for show? What was the Italian's relationship with God? And why would he sneak around playing hero?

Struggling with the zipper, Colleen asked a question only Holly could answer. "Why didn't you tell anyone?"

"Come here, let me do that," Holly said.

Obliging, Colleen turned her back to Holly.

"Hey, he saved our lives. I figured I owed him my silence when he asked for it." Holly pulled the zipper to the top.

The silky fabric of the dress clung to Colleen's curves and swished softly as she sat down on the bed next to Holly. "Why tell me this now?"

Holly took Colleen's hands. "Because I don't believe that he had anything to do with my uncle Max's shooting."

"Hmm." Colleen hadn't wanted to believe the good-looking Italian was capable of such evil when she'd heard he was a suspect in the mayor's shooting, either, but she hadn't anything concrete to base her gut instinct on.

And in light of the tale Holly had just told…

"I wonder what his story is?"

Holly squeezed her hand. "I knew I could count on you."

"Meaning?"

Holly wiggled her eyebrows. "I saw the way you

and he were making cow eyes at each other at the Valentine's dinner."

"Oh, please." Colleen stood to hide the heat in her cheeks. "We were not making cow eyes."

"Come on, you can't tell me you don't find him attractive."

Colleen reached to the back of her closet and grabbed a pair of black strappy sandals that she hadn't worn since her oldest brother's wedding. "So he's attractive. Big whoop. I'm not in the market for a man."

Holly's little chuckle grated on Colleen's nerves. A romantic relationship would only hinder her career. Colleen's plans for the future didn't include risking her heart. She'd tried that once in college and the constant worry and concern she'd felt took her focus away from journalism. Now that she was moving up in her chosen profession, she had no interest in anything romantic.

Holly's intent gaze captured Colleen's attention. "In all seriousness, would you investigate him for me? I need to know what's up with him before I tell anyone about what happened."

Colleen held out her hand to help Holly from the bed. "I'll see what I can do. But I can't promise I won't report what I find."

Holly's mouth quirked. "Can you promise to tell me first so I can prepare Jake?"

"You should tell him anyway."

"I know." Distress entered Holly's eyes. "I will. But I want all the facts before I say anything. You know your brother, he'll want all the details."

Colleen smiled. "That *is* true."

Holly preceded Colleen into the hall. As Colleen pulled her bedroom door shut behind her she thought about Alessandro Donato.

Tall, dark and mysterious.

The quintessential widower playboy, or so the rumors went. Hero in disguise or con man with an agenda?

She'd give the charming Italian the benefit of the doubt, since he'd protected Holly and Jake when they'd needed it.

But if Alessandro Donato was up to no good, she'd nail his hide to the wall all over the front page of the *Sentinel* regardless of how attractive she found him.

Alessandro Donato had a vow to fulfill. A vow to rid the world of drug dealers. Such people had cost him his family.

From his vantage point on the opposite side of trendy Fourth Street, he surveyed the bustling crowd making their way toward the door of the Colorado Springs Impressionist Museum for the opening of the Monet, Manet and Renoir collection.

He tugged on the stiff bow tie at his neck, wishing he'd thought to bring his own tux from his home in Italy.

But he'd had no way of knowing he'd still be here on this crisp May night. He'd thought that with the death of Baltasar Escalante, known drug lord, his time in Colorado Springs would have ended long ago and he'd have moved on to another assignment.

But against all logic, Escalante hadn't died when his plane went down and now had resurfaced back in this thriving community.

Only, Alessandro couldn't ID him.

His sources were confident that Escalante had had plastic surgery, so the drug lord could be any one of the men in this town. He could even be here tonight.

At the door to the museum Alessandro showed his invitation and was admitted with a cursory nod from the burly doorman.

Once inside, Alessandro took stock of the situation, noting the exits, the windows and the corridor leading to the offices where the staff of the museum worked. He'd only lived this long because he never took anything for granted.

To his right, a young, fresh-faced girl took coats and wraps from the glittering partygoers. He moved forward into the heart of the museum. Gleaming blond hardwood floors shone with a high gloss, picking up the effervescence of the crystal chandeliers.

Several benches were arranged in strategic positions, giving patrons places to sit while they contemplated the works of art on the walls. Classical pieces that attracted a huge crowd. Alessandro had to give the curator credit for securing such masterpieces.

A waiter laden with trays of savory appetizers paused and offered his fare to Alessandro.

"No, *grazie,*" he murmured as his gaze snagged on the museum's curator, Dahlia Sainsbury.

She moved with lethal grace, like a feline on the prowl. Her tall, elegant frame was draped in a signature Chanel dress of soft pink, which emphasized her pale, almost translucent skin.

As usual her dark-as-night hair was sleekly pulled back into a fancy twist at the base of her neck. Her ruby-red lips spread into a slight smile that didn't reach her sultry eyes.

Her beauty left him cold, and it had nothing to do with his vow never again to be romantically involved with a woman. No, he suspected Dahlia's beauty covered a heart of deceit.

Alessandro made his way through the crowd toward Dahlia. His instincts had been on full alert for some time now, warning him that she had something to do with Escalante. Alessandro had found a strong tie, one he hoped would lead him to the man responsible for the escalating drug trade in Colorado. The man most likely behind the shooting of Mayor Maxwell Vance.

Derisive anger shot through Alessandro. Some people thought that he had had something to do with his uncle's shooting. Ridiculous.

"Nice show tonight, Miss Sainsbury. Your gala is a fine success," Alessandro said as he halted and forced himself not to choke on the cloyingly sweet perfume permeating the air around the evening's hostess.

"So glad you approve, Mr. Donato," she responded in a clipped British accent that eerily mirrored that of another of Escalante's cohorts.

Alistair Barclay: the British hotel tycoon and Diablo crime syndicate kingpin who'd made a deal with the drug cartel run by Escalante. Together they'd used Barclay's luxury hotel business as a cover for their dirty dealings.

But through the dedicated efforts of various law-enforcement individuals and private citizens, the crime organization had been dismantled. Barclay had gone to prison and Escalante disappeared.

Recently Barclay had turned up dead in his prison cell. Alessandro was sure that Escalante was behind the assassination.

"I'd be interested in how you acquired such remarkable pieces for the exhibition," Alessandro said, focusing his mind on the task at hand.

She arched a dark, winged brow. "Ah, so that is why you called me earlier this week. I apologize that

I was unavailable. I also understand you were here yesterday while we were setting up. Do accountants for…what is it you do again?"

One side of his mouth lifted. Not for a second did he believe she'd forgotten. "I'm an accountant with the European Union."

"Ah, yes. The European Union. What would an accountant do with such knowledge?"

"You'd be surprised at the connections I have."

A sly look entered her eyes. "Connections that I might find useful?"

He leaned in closer and lowered his voice, dropping the bait. "Connections you might find profitable."

She inclined her head. "I like the sound of that. Punch?" she asked, stopping a waiter as he passed with a tray of crystal glasses filled with a colorful concoction.

Without waiting for his answer she handed him a glass. "To your health and to a future business relationship."

Over the rim of the punch-filled glass he met Dahlia's dark gaze. He suppressed the shudder that ran through him.

Somehow he felt that he'd just sold a piece of his soul. Or at least put it in hock.

Colleen felt bare in the little black tank-style dress that Holly had declared she must wear since she couldn't wear it herself. Colleen clutched the sheer blue wrap that her mother had given her tighter around her shoulders as she trailed behind her brothers, Jake and Adam, and their wives into the museum.

"Easy, now," Jake cooed to his pregnant wife, as they made their way inside.

"Honestly, you'd think I was about to give birth this instant the way you're hovering, Jake," Holly gently chided, even as she leaned on his arm.

Colleen stifled a smile, noting that Adam was just as solicitous to Kate, as well.

She was happy for both her brothers. Each had found the love of their hearts. Their soul mates. Colleen didn't have time for soul mates or any type of mate. Her life was about getting the next story and that was the only reason she'd agreed to come to this spectacle tonight.

Her editor wanted his people on the lookout for the next scoop. Well, she could only hope there'd be something to snag her interest here; all the town's most prominent citizens were attending. But she wasn't into society pieces. She much preferred gritty hard news.

"Ladies," her older brother Adam said, indicating the coat check.

Colleen frowned. "I'll just hang on to this, thanks."

Holly bumped up next to her and whispered none too softly, "Chicken."

Colleen gritted her teeth at the dual grins her brothers flashed her way.

Being the baby sister of the Montgomery brothers hadn't made for an easy childhood. Colleen had tagged along, wanting to be a part of that special world that only boys could roam. She'd long ago realized that the only way she'd get the appreciation and approval she craved was to be the best at whatever she did and not let being female hold her back.

That was why wearing a clingy shift that revealed her shoulders and showed off her calves left her feeling awkward and self-conscious. But she wasn't a chicken.

She slipped the wrap from her shoulders and handed it to Adam. He whistled between his teeth. "Maybe you better leave it on."

"Be nice," admonished his wife, Kate. "She looks lovely."

Colleen caught the dubious glance her brothers exchanged and bit her lip, wishing now she'd stuck to her pantsuit.

"*Lovely* is not quite the right word," said Jake. He reached forward and tucked a lock of hair behind Colleen's ear. "I'd say *beautiful* is the right one."

Colleen blinked as sudden tears burned her eyes. She couldn't remember her brother ever saying something so…flattering.

Adam hugged her. "I think our baby sister's grown into a woman. Finally."

His words warmed her like the first rays of sun on a cold winter's morn even as she punched him in the arm for his teasing.

"Okay, boys. Leave your sister alone," Kate said in her no-nonsense nurse voice. Then she hooked her arm through Adam's. "Shall we go in and see these paintings we've heard so much about?"

Jake slipped his arm around Holly's expanding waist and guided her in. Adam and Kate followed. Colleen waited a moment and took a few deep breaths.

She smiled and nodded hello to several people as they filed in. She waved to Reverend Gabriel Dawson from Good Shepherd Christian Church and his wife, Susan, who ran the shelter in town, as they entered.

As she started forward she heard her name called. She turned to find Sam and Jessica Vance walking toward her.

"Hey, Sam. Jessica." Sam's wavy dark-brown hair was subdued with a bit of gel, and his tall, muscular frame filled out his tuxedo nicely. Beside him, Jessica, his wife of a year, fairly glowed in her silver floor-length dress and upswept hair.

"You've got a story idea for me?" Colleen eyed Sam with hope.

Several times Sam had brought ideas for stories to her attention. Stories that needed the sort of investigating the police didn't have the manpower for.

"We're still working on the arsonist cases. Haven't had any breaks. You turn up anything?"

She shook her head. "I know Chief O'Brien had something to do with the hospital fire but I haven't nailed down what yet."

Sam nodded in agreement. "So far we've got nothing to hold him on."

"You know, I keep thinking that somehow the fires at Travis's and Quinn's businesses are connected to the hospital fire. I'm working on putting the pieces together."

Interest sparked in Sam's eyes. "Keep me posted on anything you come up with."

"I will. Enjoy the exhibition," Colleen replied and then excused herself.

She walked into the main area of the museum and looked around in awe at all the glittering ladies and well-dressed gentlemen. She felt like a fake, all dressed up as though she was one of these people.

This wasn't her. She liked khakis and loafers, not these black torture devices squeezing her feet.

"Hello, Colleen. Enjoying yourself?"

She turned toward the older woman who had stepped up beside her. "Lidia, hello. I just arrived. This is very impressive."

Lidia Vance, Mayor Maxwell Vance's wife, nodded in agreement. She wore a stunning red two-piece outfit that accentuated her olive skin and dark eyes. Italian by birth, Lidia had come to this country as Max's young bride back in the sixties. "I wish Max were here to see this."

"How is the mayor doing?"

Max Vance had been shot, but luckily not killed. His attacker was still at large.

Colleen had a hard time fitting Alessandro into the role of assassin. He was more the playboy type, not one to dirty his hands. But—impressions could be deceiving.

There was no mistaking he held an appeal that few women—except herself, of course—could resist. Like a movie star come to visit in their small community, he attracted attention.

Her sources had informed her that Donato had been hanging around the museum lately. He'd sat next to Dahlia Sainsbury, the museum's curator, at the Valentine's Day dinner. Not that Colleen had paid much attention or had an emotional reaction to the pair. It hadn't mattered to her in the least. But now... what connection did they have?

"Max is improving every day. The doctor says he'll be able to come home soon to recuperate."

Refocusing on the conversation, Colleen said, "That's wonderful. I'm sure Dad will be happy to hear that." Frank Montgomery and Maxwell Vance were lifelong friends and godparents to each other's eldest children.

Lidia smiled. "Tell your father hello for me. I know Max would welcome another visit."

"I'll let him know. I'm surprised my parents aren't here yet." Her parents were still heavily involved in community affairs even though Frank's term as mayor had long since passed.

Lidia patted her arm and moved away to talk to an older couple bedecked in jewels and finery.

Colleen looked for her editor and for the newspaper's photographer but didn't see either. She'd wait until they arrived before she started interviewing the guests. This kind of event wasn't her normal gig, but Al Crane, her editor, had insisted she attend and conduct interviews because her family knew everyone in town and they'd all talk to her.

She wasn't sure that was true, but she did want to ask the new curator about Alessandro Donato and his interest in the museum. She wandered over to a sand-colored exposed brick wall that made an elegant backdrop for Monet's "Poppy Field Near Giverny." She liked the vibrant hues: reds, blues and greens.

She moved along the wall inspecting other works by Monet when a strange awareness brushed over her. She stilled.

Slowly, she turned and scanned the room. Her gaze landed on a tall, black-haired man. Her breath hitched when she realized Alessandro Donato was staring at her. His dark, unreadable eyes conveyed a message she had trouble believing.

Even though her brothers had stated she looked beautiful tonight, Alessandro's expression made her feel beautiful.

Which was bad, *very* bad, because even if she had time for a relationship, he was the wrong kind of man to get goofy over. She wouldn't give up her independence for a playboy, no matter what, so how he saw her or made her feel was irrelevant.

Then why did she have the crazy urge to run and hide?

TWO

"Exquisite, isn't she?"

"*Sì, bellissima*," Alessandro murmured to Dahlia, his gaze riveted on the vision that had walked in only moments ago.

Colleen Montgomery.

How could this feminine beauty standing on the other side of the room be the tough-as-nails investigative reporter he'd come to admire?

Colleen's writing was witty and informative as well as thought-provoking. And the times they'd interacted, such as at the Valentine's Day dinner, he'd enjoyed her feisty personality and charming wit.

He felt Dahlia's hard stare. Alessandro blinked and realized with embarrassing clarity that he'd lost track of the conversation with the museum's curator and his only lead to Escalante. "*Scusa,* you were saying?"

Her red-as-blood lips curled. "The painting."

He glanced at the portrait of a woman standing on a hillside with a parasol. The painting had a wistful feel to the lines and strokes of the brush.

"Ah, *sì*. A masterpiece." He handed his still-full glass of punch to a passing waiter. "Miss Sainsbury, will you excuse me *un momento?*"

The knowing look in Dahlia's eyes as she gazed from him to the corner of the room where Colleen now studiously inspected a Renoir led him to believe his distraction had been quite obvious.

And it was a distraction he didn't need, because he had a drug lord to bring down.

"Of course, Mr. Donato. I'm sure we'll have plenty of time to talk business at a later date."

Alessandro hesitated. He'd come to the museum tonight to insinuate himself into Dahlia's life as a path to Escalante. He should stick close to her, but if he couldn't concentrate he'd screw up. Screwing up was not an option after what had happened to Paola.

He bowed slightly and moved away, slowly and methodically making his way toward Colleen. He'd talk with her and get her out of his system so he could get back to his real purpose: finding Escalante and taking him down, once and for all.

"Buona sera, bella signorina."

Colleen blinked as Alessandro Donato took her

hand and placed a light kiss on the knuckles. Sparks shot up her arm. "Good evening to you too, Mr. Donato."

She tilted her chin up in an effort to dispel the way the smooth cadence of his oh-so-pleasing accent caressed her senses, much as his lips caressed her fingers.

"Please, call me Alessandro," he said, a gentle smile touching his well-formed lips.

Her throat suddenly dry, Colleen swallowed. "Alessandro."

Saying his name aloud felt strange and thrilling. The name rolled off her tongue in such a delightful way, making her aware of a threat she hadn't anticipated.

This man affected her in ways she'd only experienced around him. With every interaction they'd shared, the effect had intensified.

It made her nervous. She didn't like to be nervous. Nervousness was a weakness she'd learned to overcome in order to pursue the gritty stories that would one day propel her career to new heights.

"Lovely party, no?"

"Yes, it is."

Feeling slightly off balance when she gazed into his eyes, she glanced around, hoping to find some equilibrium, and spotted her parents entering the room.

The former mayor of Colorado Springs looked

handsome in his dark tuxedo with his shocking-white hair and bushy eyebrows. Her mother wore a floral tea-length dress in vivid shades of coral that brought extra color to her rosy complexion.

Fondness for her parents tightened Colleen's chest. Her mother's bright eyes and warm smile made anyone who came in contact with her feel special.

Colleen met her mother's gaze and saw a question in her pale blue eyes: why was her only daughter talking to a man suspected of shooting his uncle?

Colleen gave a slight shrug as if to say "so what?" Her mother would understand how little stock Colleen took in the rumor mill. So often she'd proven the gossips wrong when she'd investigated a story.

She turned her gaze back to the man standing beside her. The knowing look in his dark eyes made her sense he'd somehow interpreted the exchange between mother and daughter correctly.

"Your mother is protective, no?"

His words confirmed her thoughts. "Yes. I'm her only daughter and you're basically a stranger, even though you've been in town off and on for over a year now. Still, even your aunt Lidia doesn't seem to know you well."

She studied him, liking his dark wavy hair and the aristocratic lines to his jaw. His soulful eyes could be hard and demanding yet turn so charming and compelling that her heart pounded with a rapid beat.

He'd said he was an accountant. He certainly didn't come across like any number cruncher she'd ever met. Superhero, Holly had said. Determination to uncover his secrets slid into place. "What is it exactly you do for the European Union again?"

A slow smile tipped the corners of his mouth upward. "I'm gathering information to bring back to Europe on the feasibility of opening a branch of the E.U. Bank in Colorado Springs."

"What kind of information?" She'd heard her father and Max talking about how they'd yet to see any results from Alessandro's work.

"Information that will further transatlantic economic integration and enhance the flow of investments as well as trade between the E.U. and the U.S."

"That sounds like a party line to me," Colleen stated as her reporter's instincts kicked into gear. "Does such information include art?"

"Scusi?"

"I've heard from sources that you've taken an interest in the museum. And its new curator," she commented, thinking of the brunette he'd been talking to when she walked in.

She hadn't missed the way they'd stood close together, as if they were involved romantically. Perhaps that was why he'd been hanging around. Why did a bubble of disappointment lodge itself in her chest?

He arched a brow. "Really? You are checking up on me, *bella?* I'm flattered."

A heated flush flamed in her cheeks. "People talk. Especially about a mysterious newcomer."

"Is that what I am to you, *bella?* Mysterious?" His dark eyes probed her as if he wanted to see deep inside her where she held her own private thoughts.

She rubbed at the sudden goose bumps prickling her arms. "I think you're a man with much to hide."

"For you, *cara mia,* I would gladly tell all my secrets."

"Yeah, right."

Not for one second did she believe him, but his smooth-as-silk tone and roguish smile still made little butterflies take flight in her stomach.

She lifted her chin. "I've heard that Italian men are dreadful flirts. You are very accomplished, indeed."

He chuckled, a deep sound that penetrated all the way to her heart. "What a delight you are, Colleen."

Unaccountably pleased by his words, she sought to bring some reality to the situation. "I doubt my brothers would agree with you," she replied as she caught sight of her two brothers standing side by side, glaring at them.

She smiled. They both shook their heads, clearly

indicating they didn't approve of the person she was talking to.

Alessandro followed her gaze with his own. "Ah, the protective Montgomery brothers."

"What can I say? Do you have family besides your aunt Lidia?" she asked, needing to turn the conversation back to him.

There was a story here. She wanted to unravel the mystery of this intriguing man so he'd no longer hold any appeal for her. Besides, she'd promised Holly.

"What is family? Only those whose blood you share? Or those who stand by you in time of need?"

She wasn't sure how to respond to that, but she saw something flicker in his eyes, something dark and painful, and she fought the urge to reach out to him. She had no experience in offering comfort to anyone, let alone to a man who was not family.

"Family can be both of those things. Family comes through connection. Whether through blood or friendship. Or through the bond of faith."

His expression softened. "Ah, *sì*. Faith. You believe deeply in God, no?"

"Yes. Very deeply."

"Because you were raised to believe."

"I was raised to believe, but that's not why I believe."

"Tell me, then, why do you believe?"

"Because without faith in God there is no hope."

"So is that what keeps you going, even when you investigate the travesties of the world? When you report about an abused wife whose life has become a nightmare at the hands of the one man she should trust? When you report on the drugs and the crimes perpetuated by evil men? Is it hoped that God will deliver justice? Where is the justice for the victims?"

Surprised by his passionate words, Colleen laid a hand on his arm. "God is faithful all the time," she said simply. "I don't understand God, can't fathom why the bad things in life are allowed to happen. All I can do is put my faith in the only One who does know."

Alessandro covered her hand with his. The warmth of his palm against the back of her hand made her toes curl inside her pointed black sandals. "I admire your steadfastness," he said.

His admiration was pleasing, not to mention the tender expression in his dark eyes. If she weren't careful, she could get used to having him around.

A commotion near the entrance interrupted the moment and common sense rushed in. Colleen extracted her hand. *Having him around?* What was she thinking? Obviously, she wasn't.

She didn't have time for such things. She needed to stay focused on her job.

Raised voices drew her attention. She turned to see Fire Chief Neil O'Brien push past the burly doorman.

"I've a right to be here, just as everyone else does," Neil said, his words slightly slurred.

"Not in this condition, you don't," the doorman replied and made a grab for Neil's arm. Neil dodged and continued forward, his gaze scanning the crowd, obviously looking for someone.

He looked even more haggard and worn than he had the last time Colleen had seen him, at the fire station when she'd confronted him about his gambling debts. His hair was mussed and his brown eyes bloodshot. A generous amount of weight had settled around his middle.

Colleen guessed his gambling was getting to him. She felt bad for his pregnant wife, Mary, and thankful that she wasn't here to witness the spectacle her husband was making of himself.

Neil drew up short when he met Colleen's gaze. He pointed a shaky finger at her. *"You."*

Not one ever to run from a challenge, she stepped forward. "Chief O'Brien."

"Because of you, people are saying I had something to do with the hospital fire. I told you I didn't. But you couldn't leave it alone."

"I don't for a second believe Lucia was negligent that day. My instincts tell me you're hiding something and I'm going to prove it. And if what I wrote in my article cast suspicion elsewhere, then so be it."

Colleen was aware that every person in the museum was watching, and she was even more conscious of the fact that Alessandro had come to stand behind her as if he were guarding her, protecting her.

The thought should have annoyed her. She always hated it when her brothers took that he-man stance. But having Alessandro standing watch over her made her feel secure inside.

"It didn't cast suspicion elsewhere. It cast it on me and I have enough to deal with without your vigilante journalism destroying my life." He swayed, but jerked away from Sam's steadying hand.

"It looks to me as if you're destroying your life quite nicely all by yourself," Colleen retorted, feeling sympathetic toward his wife and unborn child. "You need some help, Chief."

"I don't need anything from you people." He turned on his heel and stormed toward the entrance.

At the archway he stopped and yelled, "You'll get yours, missy. One of these days, you'll get yours. I'll see to it." Then he banged out the door.

His threat rang hollow, just like other threats she'd received before from those whom she'd upset with her candid and factual stories.

Concerned that Neil would end up doing something stupid like driving while intoxicated, Colleen took a step forward to follow him, but Alessandro's hand cupping her elbow stopped her.

"No, *bella*. You must let him deal with his mistakes on his own."

"But he shouldn't be allowed to wander the streets in his condition." She stared up into Alessandro's handsome face.

"You have such a generous heart." He released her elbow and stepped away. "Your family," he said before melting into the crowd.

Colleen took a steadying breath as her family gathered around her, making sure she was all right. After assuring everyone she was okay and that they should resume their evening, she looked around for Alessandro.

She caught a glimpse of him as he disappeared down the corridor that led to the curator's office. And the curator was nowhere in sight. Just what was the relationship between Alessandro and Dahlia Sainsbury?

But more importantly, what was this funny ache in the middle of Colleen's chest? It couldn't be jealousy, could it? Absurd.

Colleen walked over to her editor, Al Crane, who was talking to Dr. Robert Fletcher and his wife, Pamela. "Good evening, Doctor Fletcher, Mrs. Fletcher."

"How are you feeling, Colleen?" asked Dr. Fletcher. He was a tall man and still athletic in build, though his light-brown hair was thinning out. Humor always sparkled in his blue eyes.

"Good, thank you."

When Colleen had been injured during the hospital explosion a few months ago, Dr. Fletcher had been her doctor. "Do you mind if I borrow Al for a moment?"

Colleen pulled Al aside. "There's a story in Alessandro Donato."

"What kind of story?" Al asked around the unlit cigar hanging perpetually from between his lips.

At five feet eight inches, Al was paunchy and crabby and tough. Colleen liked him because he didn't give an inch and always demanded the best.

She shook her head. "Not sure yet. But there's something there."

Al narrowed his brown eyes. "Seems to me you two were getting pretty chummy before ol' Neil came blasting in."

"I was questioning him. Trying to get some background information. He was not forthcoming," Colleen replied, thinking of his words about God and justice. Not the information she'd been after, but interesting just the same. What had hardened his heart toward God?

She wouldn't admit to her editor the emotional roller-coaster ride she'd just been on, courtesy of Alessandro Donato. Alessandro had evoked curios-

ity, excitement, longing and an odd sense of rightness in her when they were together. Strange how
someone she barely knew could do that to her.

"It seems to me Neil might be a better option. Your
articles on the recent fires have him hiding. Far as I
know, this is the first time he's emerged since the
bombing at the hospital. I don't like the way he threatened you."

Colleen scoffed. "Empty words. I'm not putting
Neil on the back burner, believe me. But I want to
see what I can find out about Donato. There's something he's hiding."

Crane's bushy eyebrows rose. "You think he has
anything to do with the recent drug activity going on?"

She shrugged. "Don't know."

She couldn't picture Alessandro participating in
drug trafficking. The drug trade seemed too smarmy
for such a sophisticated man, but then stranger things
had happened. And not all criminals looked the part.
Nor did all superheroes.

Crane snagged a crab puff from a passing waitress
and popped it into his mouth. He chewed for a
moment then said, "You get the scoop on Donato and
the growing drug business in town and I'll give you
a raise."

Excitement jittered through her veins and she
grinned.

"I'll hold you to that, Crane."

He grunted and moved away to catch up with the young woman carrying the tray of appetizers. She watched him stuff two into his mouth and swipe two more. How he could eat around that disgusting cigar she didn't know.

Her mind focused on the budding story in her head. She could see the headlines in her mind. Mystery Man Revealed. Drug Trade Unraveled.

A flash of pale pink caught her gaze. Dahlia was returning from her offices, carrying a glass of punch. Alessandro wasn't with her. This would be a good opportunity to ask Dahlia about the elusive Signor Donato.

Colleen started forward and realized Dahlia was making a beeline straight to her. They met in the middle of the room.

"Miss Sainsbury, this is a lovely event," Colleen said by way of easing into a conversation.

"Thank you, dear. Punch?" She handed the crimson liquid to Colleen.

"Uh, sure." Colleen accepted the cool glass. "You've certainly worked wonders in the short time you've been here. How long has it been now?"

Dahlia waved a hand. "One loses track of time when putting together a new project."

"Where were you before coming here?"

Dahlia's expression tightened slightly. "Europe."

"Ah, so is that where you met Alessandro Donato?"

"How do you like your punch?" Dahlia asked, completely ignoring the question.

"I haven't tried it yet." It looked syrupy sweet.

"Please do. I just made a new batch and would like your opinion," Dahlia purred.

"You made this? I thought that was what the caterers were for."

Dahlia's lips thinned. "I keep tight control over everything. That's what makes me successful. Drink. Please."

Colleen lifted the glass to her lips. The sugary scent wafting up made her nose twitch. She grimaced as she opened her mouth to take a sip.

"There you are," a familiar masculine voice said from Colleen's right just as a hard body slammed into her shoulder, knocking the glass from her hand and sending it to the floor with a sickening crash.

Dahlia screeched as she jerked back, avoiding the mess. Colleen jumped away, managing to only get a few sticky drops on her shins and the tops of her black shoes.

Glaring at Mr. Tall, Dark and Suave next to her, she said, "What are you doing?"

Alessandro gave her a charming smile. "*Mi scusi!* I must have tripped."

Colleen narrowed her eyes. "Yeah, right."

He was too graceful and too self-controlled for

her to believe that nonsense. He'd done that on purpose. But why?

The sharp edge to Dahlia's tone when she instructed the wait staff to clean up the mess clearly conveyed her irritation.

"Miss Sainsbury, I may have a potential buyer for one of the paintings. Could we discuss it?" Alessandro asked.

One side of Dahlia's red lips curled. Her eyes were cold as she gave Colleen a final glance before taking his offered arm. "Indeed."

They walked away leaving Colleen to stare after them. So much for questioning Dahlia or Alessandro any further. Anger boiled in her blood.

To be made a spectacle of and then to be so easily abandoned did not sit well. Oh, yes. She was definitely going to uncover that man's secrets, even if it was the last thing she ever did.

THREE

Alessandro thought fast and spoke just as quickly, coming up with a cover story of an unnamed buyer wanting to have one of the exhibition's paintings at an astronomical price. He could see Dahlia was taking in the story at face value. There was no buyer, but he'd fork out the money himself if he needed to.

Anything to keep Dahlia from whatever mischief she had intended for Colleen.

Alessandro had seen Dahlia slip into her office while Neil O'Brien had drawn everyone's attention. As soon as Alessandro could, he'd left Colleen's side to spy on Dahlia.

Through the partially open doorway of her office, he'd heard her on the phone telling someone that, yes, it would be done, just give her a few minutes. And then she'd hung up and taken a small vial from her desk drawer and poured the contents into a glass of punch. He'd hidden in the shadows when she'd left. He'd slowly followed, wondering what she was up to.

His heart had nearly stopped when he saw her hand the glass to Colleen. He'd known he had to stop Colleen from drinking the tainted punch and the only feasible way to do so without giving up his own cover was to knock the glass from her hand.

He'd hate for anything bad to happen to Colleen. He liked her—more than he had any woman in a very long time.

Not since Paola. His heart squeezed at the thought of the woman who'd broken his heart so many years ago.

He welcomed the pain as a reminder that no matter how much he liked and admired Colleen Montgomery, she was off-limits.

He wasn't looking for a relationship.

Only for justice.

Colleen made excuses to her family that she needed to go home and clean the punch off herself, but really she wanted to get started researching Donato and Sainsbury.

She left the museum, hailed a cab and was soon home in the house she'd grown up in. Once inside the two-story ranch built in the 1940s, Colleen stepped out of her shoes, left them by the front door and then vaulted up the stairs to the guest room in the back where she'd taken up residence ever since she'd given up her downtown apartment and moved back in with her parents to save money.

It was only a temporary arrangement, but she couldn't bring herself to stay in her old bedroom with its purple walls and posters catering to her childhood whims. Living in a shrine to her youth would be too weird. She'd planned to redecorate her old room, but hadn't as of yet found time.

Once in the guest room, she changed into light-weight stretch pants and a T-shirt, pulled her hair up into a ponytail and then fired up her laptop computer.

With the marvel of modern technology, she'd have access to all sorts of information on Donato. And luckily she knew several reporters in Europe who would be willing to do a little footwork for her.

She settled in and started digging into the life of Alessandro Donato.

Alessandro was glad to see Colleen leave, but he hated that he had the urge to follow her home to make sure she arrived safely.

As it was, he'd watched her get in the cab without harm and that would have to do for now. Without the distraction of Colleen's presence, he could concentrate on initiating Dahlia's trust.

Dahlia had led him to an alcove near the swinging doors that closed off the caterers from the party.

"Tell me, Mr. Donato, would your buyer be willing to come to Colorado Springs and meet with me?"

"*Sì*, that could be arranged."

Out of habit he moved to stand with his back toward the wall so he could see any approaching threats.

Dahlia laid a hand on his arm. "Good. You'll get back to me with a time?"

"*Sì*, yes." Alessandro would contact his boss and have someone arrange to pose as an art buyer.

A piercing scream split the air.

The noise came from behind the swinging doors.

"Stay put," Alessandro said to Dahlia, as he left her to charge through the doors.

A sobbing waitress was trying to explain to another waiter what had made her scream. Alessandro took her hands. "Shh. Breathe, *signorina*. Slowly, now. What has caused your tears?"

Behind him, the swinging doors banged open as Sam Vance stormed in, followed closely by the Montgomery brothers and Al Crane.

"I heard a scream. Is someone hurt?" Sam demanded.

The girl hanging on to Alessandro's hands hiccupped and then pointed out the back door. "I think… he's dead."

Alessandro beat Sam out the door. Seeing Neil O'Brien face down on the ground, Alessandro hung back as Sam bent to check the pulse of the man lying prone in the alleyway, a dark stain spreading across his back.

"He's dead," Sam confirmed.

Sam secured the crime scene and placed a call for forensics. The burly doorman ushered all the bystanders back inside, where they were instructed to wait because the police would need to ask questions since they were all potential witnesses.

Alessandro observed Dahlia's less-than-horrified expression as she assured those around her that the museum would be open for visiting as soon as the next day.

As the CSI techs and medical examiner arrived, Alessandro stayed on the fringes of the activity. After combing the scene for clues, the CSI team released the victim. They rolled Neil over and placed his body in a black bag before loading him onto a gurney and taking him away.

Alessandro watched Sam bend down and with the end of a pencil pick something up. A large lump formed in Alessandro's chest when he realized the object of Sam's inspection was the blue scarf Colleen had been wearing when she'd first walked into the museum.

Colleen stayed up all night, tapping her resources for information on the mysterious Alessandro Donato. She'd e-mailed a friend at immigration asking for information on Alessandro's visa, because knowing where the visa originated and when it expired could be helpful.

The information supplied had led her to Fabriano, Italy.

She contacted a former classmate who lived in Rome and had her check hospital records in the small town in the center of the country.

A few hours later, the information she received back stunned her. Not only had Alessandro been born in that small Italian community, but so had his child. A little girl.

The knowledge hit her like a physical blow. It was one thing to think of Alessandro as a playboy but another to know that there was a woman in his life.

"A daughter," she muttered as she typed in the information in the spreadsheet she used as a tool for gathering notes for her articles.

She could picture a raven-haired feminine version of Alessandro running around with mischief in her dark eyes and a grin on her face.

The image tightened something unfamiliar in her chest. She frowned.

Children were for other people, not her. She didn't have time in her life for the ties of an immediate family. Yet…she couldn't shake the strange feeling or the image. She hoped that if she slept, she'd be able to banish the sudden abnormal longing for a family of her own.

She forced herself to lie down and tried the relaxation techniques she'd learned in college when she'd needed sleep in order to be attentive for her classes. Deep breathing and concentrating on letting each limb become heavy helped her to relax. Eventually she fell into a light sleep.

Colleen awoke as daylight filtered in through the slats of the blinds covering the window. Though she was not completely refreshed, her mind buzzed with alertness.

Without preamble, she went back to work. In her note file, she typed, Where's mother of child? Where's child? Is the mother his dead wife? Is Dahlia Sainsbury mother of child? If so, what are they planning? If not, is he just a playboy sniffing after a pretty face?

That last question brought her up short.

There was no question the man was suave and charming. He had the ability to make whomever he was talking to feel special. But a womanizer?

Surely she'd have heard rumors of specific liaisons if that were the case. No, whatever he was up to wasn't anything so frivolous or obvious.

"Find the child and the mother won't be far away," she muttered.

She put another request in to her Italian connec-

tion and asked that she track down the child's where-
abouts and check marriage records for Alessandro
Donato.

A knock sounded at the front door. She glanced
at the clock and realized she was alone in the house.
Her parents would have left over an hour ago.

She clicked out of her e-mail and brought up her
desktop screen saver: an ocean beach with tranquil
water and warm-looking sand. One of these days she
was going on a vacation.

She left her office and went downstairs to open
the front door. Becca Hilliard and Sam Vance stood
on the stoop.

"Hey, guys, come in." Colleen stepped back to let
them enter. It wasn't unusual for the pair of detectives to appear at her front door. Often they'd come
with leads or in hopes of gaining information on a
story she was working on.

Becca's light-brown hair was pulled back into
her usual long ponytail hanging almost to her waist.
She was dressed in navy slacks and matching jacket
over a white blouse. She smiled slightly as she
stepped into the foyer. "Hello, Colleen."

Sam passed Colleen without comment. His tall,
muscular build could be overwhelming at times, especially when he was working. His dark wavy hair
looked clean and his face freshly shaved, but Colleen
noticed the grim expression tightening his strong jaw.

"Where were you last night?" Sam asked as he looked around.

Colleen arched one eyebrow. "You saw me last night at the museum. What's up?"

Becca walked into the living room. "Are you alone?"

Wary, Colleen followed her in. "Yes."

"Where did you go after you left the museum last night?" Becca asked.

Colleen slid her gaze to Sam, who watched her with hooded eyes. She frowned. "I came here."

"Was anyone here?" Sam asked, his voice low.

"No. I heard my parents come home later."

"Where are they now?" Becca asked.

"They're at their Bible study. Every Thursday morning for the past ten years." Colleen put her hands on her hips. "What is going on?"

"Did you see Neil O'Brien after you left last night?"

Becca's softly asked question sent a ripple of concern down Colleen's spine. "No. He stormed out and that was that." She shook her head. "He was really drunk. I hope he didn't get in a car and drive like that."

"No. He didn't get into a car." Sam moved restlessly around the room.

Colleen tracked his progress. "Sam. Talk to me."

He stopped his pacing and turned to look directly in her eyes. "Do you own a gun?"

"What?" She dropped her chin. "Do I need one?"

He moved to stand right in front of her. "Colleen. Neil O'Brien was murdered last night."

Colleen staggered back a step. He was about to be a father. "Oh, poor Mary. How… What happened?"

"Someone shot him in the back," came Becca's reply.

"In the back?" Colleen's journalistic nose twitched. "I've got to get my notebook."

"Actually, Colleen, we need you to come down to the station with us."

Colleen stopped and stared at Sam as realization came at her like one of Jake's baseballs, effectively knocking the wind from her lungs. "The question about the gun…you think I…how could you…?"

Contrition showed bright in Sam's warm brown eyes. "It's just routine. You had an altercation with the man prior to his murder."

"So that makes me guilty of killing him?" she asked, her voice rising. "Sam, you've known me my whole life."

Becca stepped forward. "There's more, Colleen. We really need your cooperation."

"I'm not going anywhere," she stated.

Her mind whirled with story angles and possible suspects in Chief O'Brien's murder. She had to get out on the street and find out who had killed Neil.

"Then we'll need to read you your rights and then take you to the station," Becca said softly.

"Read me my rights?" Panic slithered up her spine. She felt as if she'd somehow walked into a B movie and wasn't able to follow the plot line. "What are you saying?"

"Colleen Montgomery, you're under arrest for the murder of Neil O'Brien...."

"What are you doing here?"

Alessandro halted at his cousin Sam's harshly asked question. He'd come to the police station as soon as he heard they'd arrested Colleen.

Not for the first time, Alessandro wished he could confide in his cousin that they were on the same side.

But he couldn't.

The fewer people privy to such information, the better. For their sakes as well as for his own.

"Colleen Montgomery had nothing to do with Neil O'Brien's death."

Sam raised a brow. "Do you have proof of this?"

Knowing his words would mean little to nothing to the detective, Alessandro stated, "Your evidence is circumstantial at best."

"That's for her lawyer to prove," Sam retorted.

Frustration tightened in Alessandro's gut. "You can't believe she did this."

Sam ran a hand through his hair. "It doesn't matter what I believe. I have to follow the law."

Not above using their familial connection, Alessandro lowered his voice and said, "Cousin, I know you have no reason to trust me. But trust yourself. You know Colleen wouldn't hurt anyone. She is being framed. Think for a moment. The articles she has been writing lately on the escalating drug trade…the fires…someone wants her stopped. And I know who it is."

Sam grabbed him by the arm and pulled him into an interrogation room and shut the door. "You better tell me what you know, *Cousin.*"

"Baltasar Escalante is not dead."

Sam gave him a droll look. "Really. And you know this…how?"

Alessandro ground his teeth together. He couldn't reveal his source of information without blowing his own cover. "You'll have to trust me."

Sam snorted. "As you said, I have no reason to trust you."

Regret for the image he'd been forced to cultivate in order to work his way closer to Escalante's people stabbed him in the chest. "I can't explain how I know. He is back."

Sam shook his head. "We'd have spotted him."

This time Alessandro shook his head. "He has had plastic surgery."

Sam scoffed. "You can't expect me to go to my superiors with this without any proof or any corroborating evidence. I'd be laughed off the force."

Sam opened the door and walked back into the hall.

Anger burned in Alessandro's chest. He had to find Escalante and bring him down before he destroyed any more lives.

Including Colleen's.

"Thank you, Jake, Adam. I love you guys." Colleen hugged each brother and sent a silent prayer of thanks heavenward for the devotion of her family.

As soon as she'd reached the police station she'd called Jake. She was confident that as an FBI agent, he would know what to do. Her brothers had arrived within the hour with a lawyer in tow.

They'd agreed to tell their parents after they had Colleen released. A terrific idea as far as she was concerned. Frank Montgomery would chew some hide inside and out as it was when he found out that Colleen had been arrested. At least this way they could protect Sam and Becca until Frank cooled down.

"That's what big brothers are for." Jake shrugged and grinned while adjusting his conservative red tie. He dressed the role of FBI agent nicely in a navy suit and black wingtip shoes. "Getting our little sister out of scrapes is what we do."

"I don't think this qualifies as a scrape," Adam said, concern clouding his eyes. As a doctor, Adam dressed more casually in tan pants and an oxford dress shirt with the sleeves rolled up.

"You're right," Jake agreed, his expression turning somber. "This was a frame. Someone's out to get you."

Colleen frowned. "Who? Why? That doesn't make any sense." Though deep inside, a nagging feeling that they were right clamored for her attention.

Obviously someone disliked her enough to want to implicate her in Neil's death. Her reporter's brain raced toward possible reasons why someone would be out to get her.

Could her suppositions that the hospital fire, the Montgomery Construction fire and the Double V Ranch fire were all somehow connected be on track? The timing of the fires had been way too coincidental and too specific to the Vance and Montgomery families. Had her report on the recent increase in drug activity since the mayor's shooting stirred some hornet's nest? But whose? The mysterious *El Jefe,* who reportedly had been contacting Escalante's old contacts? No one seemed to be able to identify the new would-be drug lord in town.

"I should have remembered to pick up my scarf when I left last night," she mused.

"Hey, don't beat yourself up for something you had no control over," Jake said.

The door to the small windowless, mirrored room opened and Craig Smith, her lawyer, walked in. His pinstripe suit and shiny black shoes made him look professional, but his youthful face made Colleen jittery. She only hoped her brother was right when he'd assured her that, though Craig was young, he was good.

Pushing up the wire-rimmed glasses that seemed to constantly be sliding down his straight nose, Craig said, "I've had a talk with the D.A. and he agrees that the evidence they have isn't enough to charge you with Neil O'Brien's murder."

"So I can go?" Colleen asked.

She couldn't wait to get home and start working on the O'Brien case. And continue her research on Alessandro, the latter for purely professional reasons. It had nothing to do with the fact that the Italian man intrigued her. She had to stay objective and report just the facts, no matter what her own personal feelings were.

Which, where Alessandro was concerned, were confusing.

She liked him, yet didn't completely trust him. But not for any real reason—she'd exonerated him in her mind from the attempt on Mayor Max's life— but she knew he was keeping secrets.

Anyone who kept their own child a secret had to be involved in something sketchy.

Craig said, "Yes. I would advise you not to leave

town, because at the moment, you're considered a 'person of interest' in the case."

"I don't have any plans to go anywhere." Colleen marched past the men and headed out the door.

Behind her she heard her brothers thanking Craig, but her gaze was captured by the tall man standing at the end of the hall, talking with Sam. Her heart plummeted. Oh, no.

She hurried toward the two men. "Sam, you can't think Alessandro had anything to do with Neil's death?" she exclaimed as she skidded to a halt.

The tender smile she received from Alessandro sent her heartbeat into overdrive. "No worries, *cara.*"

Sam snorted. "The man came to say *you* had nothing to do with Neil's murder."

Colleen blinked. "Really?"

Warmth gushed through her like water from a broken dam. She didn't know what to think of Alessandro's chivalrous actions. She gazed up at him, looked deep into his dark eyes, and for a moment the buzz of the police station dimmed.

"Thank you," she murmured.

He gave a slight nod of acknowledgement before shifting his gaze past her, effectively breaking the mesmerizing hold he'd had on her and leaving her slightly off balance.

"What's he doing here?" Adam demanded from behind her.

Colleen rolled her eyes and grimaced. Her brothers were doing the he-man routine again.

"Believe it or not, he came to defend your sister," Sam stated, clearly enjoying Colleen's discomfort, if the smirk he gave her was any indication.

Heat crept up her neck. She could just imagine the expressions on her brothers' faces. She didn't want to turn around and see the incredulity or the skepticism.

They would never believe Alessandro had come because he cared about her. Come to think of it, she didn't believe he'd come for that reason, either. So why had he?

That was a question she was determined to answer. Along with several others. But first she had to get out of here and away from the stifling, protective cover of her family. "Alessandro, would you be willing to give me a ride home?"

"What!" Jake and Adam both exclaimed.

Colleen kept her back to her brothers and waited for Alessandro to respond. His dark eyebrows rose slightly as his gaze shifted back to her.

She held her breath, hoping he'd say yes and wondering how she'd live down the embarrassment if he said no.

FOUR

Mamma mia! He'd stepped in a minefield by coming to the police station. But Alessandro couldn't seem to muster up enough panic as Colleen's blue eyes bored into his. He knew if he agreed to take her home, he'd alienate her brothers even more. And his cousin.

But it would sustain his cover as the playboy accountant.

Besides, he sensed there was more going on here than a simple ride. She obviously had something to prove to her brothers and if he could accommodate her, so be it.

It wasn't as though he had any romantic feelings, despite his admiration of her. He had no plans to go down that particular path again.

"Bella?" Alessandro offered her his arm.

Relief shone bright in her gaze. She slipped her hand in the crook of his elbow. "Thank you."

She turned to her brothers. "I'll talk with you later."

"You can't leave with him," Jake sputtered.

"See ya." She tugged at Alessandro's arm as she moved forward.

Amused, Alessandro could only give the three men glaring at him a shrug that said "What can I say? She wants me." *"Ciao."*

"Colleen Montgomery, you come back here," Adam demanded.

Colleen's steps quickened and Alessandro lengthened his stride. *"Bella,* I think you've made your brothers angry."

"They'll get over it," she said as he pushed open the glass doors for her. She didn't let go of his arm as they stepped into the sunshine. "Where's your car?"

"There." He pointed to the small red convertible parked at the curb.

Her eyes widened and then she grinned. "Cool."

"You are such a delight, *bella,*" he said as he opened the door for her to slide into the passenger seat. Her enthusiasm lifted his mood.

He rounded the car to the driver's side and climbed in, then secured his seat belt and turned to her. "Home?"

"Breakfast?" Her blue eyes twinkled.

Ah. So there *was* more to this than a mere ride.

"Whatever you wish," he stated.

He gunned the engine and sped away from the police station. In his rearview mirror he saw her brothers had come out the doors and were watching them drive away. The urge to put his arm around her shoulders was more than he could resist. "Where to?"

She glanced at his outstretched arm lightly resting across the tops of her shoulders. "The Stagecoach. Of course."

With a grin, he drove through the morning traffic and turned onto South Cascade Avenue in the heart of downtown Colorado Springs. With over a half a million in population in the metro area, the town bustled with activity. Between residents going about their everyday lives and tourists come to enjoy the beauty of the town nestled beneath Pikes Peak, the downtown offered something for everyone.

For the avid reader, the stunning branch of the Pikes Peak Library District was within walking distance from countless relaxing reading spots. Many times over the years Colleen had spent time in one of the many lush parks, working on a story or sitting in a coffee shop among the thriving businesses and apartment buildings of the main thoroughfare.

After removing his arm from around her, Alessandro slipped the car into a parking spot in front of the charming red barnlike structure that claimed to serve the best apple pie this side of the Rockies.

He climbed out and came around to open Colleen's door. She slipped her small, delicate hand into his as he helped her out of the car. He liked the way her skin felt so soft and velvety in his grasp.

Inside the café, Fiona Montgomery, her bright-red hair piled high on her head and her warm brown eyes sparkling, bustled forward. "Colleen, honey, how are you?"

Fiona eyed Alessandro up and down. "And you brought a friend. Lidia's nephew, right?"

Alessandro nodded and suppressed a smile at the way Fiona's tone dipped on the word *friend.* Clearly, Colleen didn't bring many *friends* to the café. And for some reason, that pleased him.

Fiona sat them at a window table and hurried away with a promise to return quickly to take their orders.

"My aunt Fiona's the best cook in town," Colleen boasted as she settled into the red vinyl seat.

"I thought my aunt Lidia was the best cook in town," he teased.

Colleen grinned. "They both are," she conceded. "Tell me about Italy. Where you grew up."

He leaned back and stretched his legs beneath the table, his knee brushing against hers. "I grew up in a small town in the center of Italia called Fabriano, most famous for the paper mills. The paper with the, as you say, watermark, was invented in Fabriano."

"Interesting. Do you have family there still?"

His gut clenched, but he answered honestly. *"Sì. Mi madre e padre."*

"And your aunt Lidia is…?"

"Older sister to *mi madre.*"

Colleen nodded and Alessandro had the distinct feeling she was working up to something. And he had no intention of revealing anything more to her than necessary. He glanced up and was relieved to see Fiona heading their way.

"So, what will it be today?" Fiona asked in her usual vivacious way.

Colleen grinned. "What do you think I want, Aunt Fiona?"

Fiona grinned back. "My famous apple pie."

"You guessed it."

Pie for breakfast. Another reason to like this woman. Alessandro held up two fingers. *"Due, per favore."*

Fiona winked. "Good choice. Two apple pies coming up."

Colleen put her elbows on the table, folded her hands and rested her chin on her knuckles. She looked so sweet and innocent that danger alarms went off in his head.

"Tell me more about your family," she said.

His family was off-limits, so instead he told her of Italy and of his hometown of Fabriano. He described the *Piazza del Comune,* the plaza in the center of town where everyone gathered after siesta.

He told her of the Gothic *Palazzo del Podestà* with its swallowtail battlements. She took it all in, her curiosity and intelligence shining in her bright eyes.

"It sounds wonderful," she said, her tone wistful.

"In the centre of the *Piazza del Comune* is a smaller version of Perugia's famous fountain. This is where the younger crowd, what is it you Americans say?…hang out."

"Did you hang out there as a teen?"

He shrugged. "*Sì.* A good place to watch the girls."

Her mouth twisted. "I can just picture you acting all cool, flirting with girls."

"It's the Italian way."

She rolled her eyes. "I think it's a universal male thing."

He raised his eyebrows. "You speak of your brothers, no?"

She made a noise in the side of her mouth. "Yes."

Fiona returned, her hands full. "Here we go, two orders of my famous apple pie," she said, as she placed two plates heaped with steaming hot apple pie and a generous side helping of vanilla ice cream on the table.

Alessandro breathed deeply, enjoying the spicy

scents of cinnamon, nutmeg and apple. "*Grazie,* Signora Fiona."

"Well, go on, taste it," she prompted.

He took a bite, savoring the tang of apples and spice of cinnamon. "Mmm, *molto bene.*"

Fiona flashed a pleased smile. "I take it that means you like."

"*Sì.*" He made a gesture of excellence with his fingers. "*Magnifica.*"

She gave a satisfied nod before moving on to another table.

"I think Aunt Fiona likes you," Colleen said around a mouthful of apple pie.

"Really?" He took a bite of the sweet confection.

Colleen nodded. "She doesn't give just anyone this big a portion," she said pointing her fork to their plates. "Can I ask you something?"

"Of course."

She dragged her fork through her ice cream, leaving long, thin tracks. "Did you have anything to do with the attack on your uncle?"

So much for the chitchat. Very deliberately, he set his fork down and looked her directly in the eye. He wanted her to see the truth in his expression as he said, "No, *bella.* I did not."

She gazed at him a moment as if trying to discern the sincerity in his words. A thoughtful expression entered her eyes. "It was weird the way you got a call just moments before the news came that he'd been shot. Brendan mentioned it to me."

He shrugged. "Coincidence."

"I don't believe in coincidence. Everything happens for a reason."

He didn't like that she would think something so bad about him. He reached across the table and took her hand. "What would I gain from hurting my uncle?"

Two lines appeared between her eyebrows. "I don't know. I guess that's what puzzles me about the suspicions running around that you had something to do with the mayor's shooting. I just don't see how you could have benefited. I don't think you had anything to do with it. I just needed to hear you say it."

Thankful that she wasn't judging him on the strength of rumors, he squeezed her hand before letting go. "I do not know my uncle well. For that matter, I don't know my aunt or cousins well. But they are family."

Her gaze narrowed. "And family is important to you?"

"*Sì.* To you, too, no?"

"Family is important." She pushed her plate away and then pierced him with her blue eyes. "If family is important to you, Alessandro, tell me why you've never mentioned you have a wife and child?"

With the force of a gale wind, the grief that

always surfaced when he thought of his wife blew over him, making him want to howl with rage.

He forced the unwanted emotions back to the dark hole in his heart.

Focusing on the moment, everything inside went on alert. He'd sensed Colleen had been working up to something; he just wasn't prepared for this. He should have known that Colleen's tenaciousness would lead her to dig into his life; she was a reporter, after all.

She posed a threat to all he'd been striving for over the last few years, as well as a threat to his family's lives.

And to her own life.

He needed to make her understand how important it was for her to stop digging, that she could be hurt or even killed for her efforts. But how did he do that without revealing the true nature of his work?

He glanced around to make sure no one was eavesdropping on their conversation. Though no one seemed overly interested in them, he couldn't be sure. He slid out of the booth and stood. Taking out his wallet and laying down some bills that would more than cover their pies, he stated, "This is neither the time nor the place, *cara,* for such discussions."

Heart racing, Colleen scrambled out of the booth. Alessandro's expression was unreadable as he placed his hand on the small of her back, the pressure warm and comforting.

She allowed him to lead her out the door. Once they were inside the car and headed toward her neighborhood, Colleen couldn't refrain any longer. "So, answer my question. Why do you claim to be a widower?"

He gave her a sidelong glance full of anger and something else that twisted her up inside. She saw a deep pain in the depths of his eyes and she fought the urge to reach out to him, to soothe the hurt there. She needed to stay objective if she wanted to uncover his secrets.

He remained silent until he pulled up in front of her parents' home. He turned off the engine and sat staring forward for a long moment.

Finally, he faced her and the fierce light in his dark eyes made her draw back, not in fear but in surprise.

"You must stay out of my personal business, Colleen. You must drop this. What you think you know is not for print."

For the second time in as many days someone was asking for the impossible. First Holly, now this man. "I can't. I'm an investigative reporter, Alessandro. This is what I do. It's who I am."

His nostrils flared with anger. "How can I make you understand that lives are in danger? If you pursue your…probing, you could destroy many lives. Including your own."

The unnamed threat in his words sent a chill down

her spine and solidified her desire to uncover the mystery surrounding this man. The challenge was always what drove her.

"Then tell me the truth," she said. "Tell me who you really are and why you're really here. And what do Dahlia Sainsbury and the museum have to do with you?"

He closed his eyes briefly as if struggling with a decision. When he opened them, the determination in his expression was almost palpable. "You must trust me, *bella*. Stop this now, before anyone gets hurt."

His gaze shifted to something beyond her shoulder, out the window. "Your parents."

She twisted in the seat to look out the passenger-side window. Sure enough, her parents, looking as though they'd stepped out of a Norman Rockwell painting, were standing on the porch. If she didn't get out soon she fully expected her father with his deep scowl would come charging down the stairs to drag her from the car to make sure she was all right.

The worried expression on her mother's face made Colleen open the door and wave a greeting to let them know all was well.

Turning back to Alessandro, she said, "I'm going to find out the truth one way or another. It would be better if you told me."

He hit the steering wheel with the flat of his hand. "No. You must let this go."

"Sorry, can't do that." She slipped out of the car and shut her door, then watched him roar away. He hadn't denied that he had a wife and child and she couldn't ignore the disappointment slashing her chest.

Okay, so he was married with a family. Big deal. She had no claim on him, so she had no right to feel anything other than curiosity.

A reporter's curiosity.

His reaction seemed over the top. He was protecting some other secret beyond having a wife and child.

What could he possibly be hiding that would make him so passionate about keeping it hidden?

Alessandro felt as if he'd gone ten rounds in a boxing ring. Colleen wouldn't give up: it wasn't in her nature. He knew that.

And in part, that was what drew him to her.

He liked the confidence and strength of character she possessed. He admired the way she went after a story and didn't let go until she had answers. He just wished she didn't view him as a story.

He entered his suite, closed the door and leaned back against it as the realization came that he wished Colleen would view him as a man.

But what good would that do either of them?

It was his job to keep secrets. It was her job to uncover them and put them on display for the world to see.

He'd somehow let her get under his skin. A dangerous thing indeed.

He stripped off his sports coat as he walked into the living room of the two-bedroom suite, and stopped when he saw his brother sitting in the plush recliner, reading a book.

As always when he was not working, his brother dressed in casual cargo pants and a T-shirt splashed with the name of the latest fad designer across the front.

Tomas looked up. "Rough day?" he asked in their native language.

"That obvious?"

"Yes. And I'm about to make it worse."

Alessandro groaned and held up a hand. "Let me at least take off my shoes and sit before you unload on me."

Tomas went back to his book, which Alessandro noted with some amusement was *Wild at Heart* by John Eldridge. His brother was always looking for ways to deepen his faith.

Alessandro had long ago given up on that endeavor.

Kicking off his shoes, he stretched out on the couch and propped his head up on the throw pillow. "All right. What's up?"

Tomas set down his book. "They want you off the case."

Alessandro closed his eyes and focused on

breathing. "No. I went over this the last time I was called in. I won't. I'm close. I can feel it."

"All the more reason for you to get out now. Let someone else take over. The higher-ups believe that your bitterness over Paola's death is going to compromise the case and lead you to do something they don't want happening."

Alessandro snorted. "Like getting rid of Escalante once and for all?" He opened his eyes. "No deal. I'm in to the end."

Tomas sat up straighter. "You're getting emotionally involved, brother. You know that makes for a bad situation."

Alessandro swung his feet off the end of the couch and stood up. "Of course I'm getting emotionally involved. Some of these people here are family."

"Not all."

"What does that mean?"

Tomas stood. "Colleen Montgomery."

Everything inside Alessandro seized with apprehension. He began to pace. "I am not getting involved with her. Emotionally or otherwise."

"Ha!" Tomas gestured in disgust. "You left the police station with her. Ate in a public restaurant."

A protective anger stirred. Alessandro narrowed his gaze. "How do you know that?"

"Our contact here in town." Tomas indicated the phone. "You need to make a phone call."

Alessandro growled with frustration and grabbed the phone. He punched in the number for his contact from memory.

On the second ring a distorted, non-gender-specific voice answered, "Falcon."

"You are not taking me off this case," Alessandro stated in English. "I made that clear already."

"We're worried your personal feelings are getting in the way."

"Personal feelings? You're right, I have personal feelings about Escalante. The man's a menace and needs to be taken down."

"I'm not talking about Escalante. I'm talking about Colleen Montgomery. You can't jeopardize the mission by becoming involved with an investigative reporter."

He scrubbed his free hand over his face. "I'm not becoming involved," he stated between clenched teeth.

He had no intention of leaving his heart vulnerable to a woman again, especially not to a strong-willed one, no matter how much he found her alluring.

"I can handle Colleen."

"Not if she takes it into her head to find out all there is about you."

Alessandro grimaced. He couldn't let on that she knew about Mia. "It will take her some time."

"You need to come in now!"

"No!" Alessandro held on to his rising frustration. "I'm close to getting Dahlia Sainsbury to trust me.

I'm sure she's in league with Escalante—I can feel it. I just need a little more time."

"And what of Colleen?"

"She's a suspect in Neil O'Brien's murder. That should keep her occupied."

"Hmm. Yes. We'll make sure it does."

Concern for Colleen arched through Alessandro, but he pushed it aside. He had to stay focused on bringing an end to Escalante and his drug trade. Colleen would be fine.

The image of Dahlia handing Colleen the tainted punch flashed in his mind. "Colleen needs protection. She's become a target of Escalante's because of her investigations."

"Stay away from Colleen Montgomery. She's no longer your worry. Get Escalante."

The phone went dead.

Although logically Alessandro knew Falcon was right—Colleen Montgomery would only jeopardize his mission—he couldn't help feeling as though he'd just lost something precious.

All the more reason for him to stay away from Colleen. She was a risk to his heart, and that was something he couldn't allow. He had no desire to go through the heartache of loss again.

No, he had to stay focused on meting out the justice that God hadn't seen fit to do.

FIVE

Three days after her arrest, Colleen stepped into the fire station much as she had a few months earlier when she'd been investigating the hospital fire; the fire at AdVance, Travis Vance's private investigation firm; and the fire at Montgomery Construction.

Back then, Battalion Chief O'Brien had been alive and intent on blaming the hospital fire on Lucia.

Colleen's articles on the not-so-seemingly random fires had helped to throw suspicion elsewhere. Namely on Chief O'Brien's head. Boy, had he been steaming mad at the museum gala.

Now the man was dead and Colleen suspected of his murder.

A career-limiting development if she'd ever heard of one. Not to mention a life-altering situation if someone were successful in framing her for Neil's murder. Her stomach bunched in a ball every time she thought about it.

"Hey, Colleen, what are you doing here?" Luke Donovan, Lucia's partner, asked as he came out of the dining room where she saw several other firefighters gathered at the long table. Luke strode toward her down the short hallway. His big football player's physique took up most of the hall. His blond crew cut looked damp, as if he'd recently showered. His jeans were worn to a faded blue and his plaid long-sleeved shirt hung partway open, revealing his T-shirt underneath.

"Doing a little investigating," she answered warily, adjusting the collar of her pink cotton blouse. Would Luke demand she leave, considering she was suspected of murdering his boss?

"Of the chief's death?"

"Yes."

He nodded, his grimace one of sympathy. "I don't blame you. Just for the record, none of us here think you had anything to do with his death."

Relief washed through Colleen. She gave Luke a grateful smile. "Thanks. I appreciate that. Is Lucia around?"

"In her cube." He indicated the direction of the office cubicles with a jerk of his head.

"See you later," she said and headed for Lucia's desk.

Her friend was busy writing on a thick notepad. Her dark, straight hair hung over one slim shoulder and spilled down her back to cover most of her striped shirt.

The cluttered work space made Colleen wince. A stuffed bear sat in one corner; several family photos lining the back wall were barely visible because yellow sticky notes with Lucia's precise handwriting covered every available smooth surface. Colleen leaned forward to read one. Objective of Fire???

"You know, I'd like an answer to that question myself," Colleen stated as she flicked a finger at the sticky note.

Lucia sat back with a small yelp. "Don't do that."

Colleen grinned. "Sorry."

"You're forgiven." Lucia's eyebrows creased. "I'd like to know how my brother could think you had anything to do with the chief's death."

Colleen shrugged. "He's just doing his job." But it still stank that he'd had to arrest her. Her stomach turned queasy, but she forced herself to stay calm. She didn't want anyone to know how upsetting she'd found the experience.

Lucia's chocolate brown eyes flashed with anger. "There are plenty of people who had reasons enough to want the chief in the grave. Me included."

Grateful for her friend's support, Colleen gave her a quick hug. "You're the best."

Hugging her back, Lucia commented, "You seem

awfully chipper for someone detained and questioned for murder."

Being hauled to the police station like a criminal in the back of squad car had been infuriating, but leaving with Alessandro in his sporty vehicle had salvaged some of the day. But she refused to voice that thought. No need to let her friend know that bit of information.

Colleen stepped away and hiked a hip on the edge of the desk. "Hey, I'm not guilty until proven otherwise. And since there isn't any proof to be found, life's good." At least she hoped it would be.

With a sly grin, Lucia shot back, "Especially when a certain handsome Italian man soundly defends you, then whisks you away to have a leisurely breakfast at the Stagecoach."

Heat crept up Colleen's neck. Lucia knew her too well *and* knew too much. "He's just a friend." And that was all he could ever be.

Lucia scoffed. "It's me you're talking to."

Colleen rolled her eyes. "You and Holly see romance in everything."

"Don't knock it until you try it," Lucia said with a wide smile.

Colleen smiled back, happy for Lucia, who'd found love with Rafe Wright, a smokejumper for the U.S. Department of Agriculture. They'd met when Rafe had saved Lucia's life in the hospital fire. For the first time, Colleen felt a twinge of envy for her friend's joy in finding a relationship that made her so happy. Did she ever become anxious? Worry that somehow it would all end and she'd be left alone and grieving like Mary? The thought was heart-wrenching and too awful to consider.

Wanting to switch to a less disconcerting topic, namely the reason she'd come to the firehouse, Colleen asked, "Could you get me into the chief's office?"

Lucia's eyebrows drew together. "Do you think you should do that, considering…"

"It's my life, my *reputation* on the line here."

Lucia nodded with understanding. "Come on."

They walked through the other cubicles toward the office of Battalion Chief O'Brien. Though his office was empty, Colleen felt a chill of foreboding run down her spine.

"Sam and Becca have already gone through the drawers and files. I don't think they found anything noteworthy," Lucia commented while rubbing her arms as if reacting to the ominous feeling as well.

Colleen moved to the desk. "I don't know what I'm looking for. Maybe something that would tell us why he was at the museum three nights ago."

"You should probably talk with Mary."

"I'm sure Sam already has," Colleen said as she opened the drawers of the desk. Nothing in them but the normal office supplies. Chief O'Brien had been meticulous with his stuff, even if he hadn't been as careful with his body.

Lucia pointed at her. "I'm sure you're right, but you, my friend, have the ability to get information out of people the police sometimes can't."

Pleased by the praise, Colleen flashed a smile as she lifted the blotter. Nothing. Slipping her hand between the blotter and its plastic cover just in case, her fingers scraped along a solid edge.

An arrow of anticipation zoomed through her as she pulled the blotter apart. A white envelope addressed in type to Mary O'Brien had been hidden in the far corner of the blotter's plastic edge.

Written by Neil in case of his death?

Colleen flipped the envelope over with the tip of a pen. The seal was broken.

"What is it?" Lucia asked as she stepped closer.

"A letter for Mary," Colleen replied. "Do you have a plastic bag or something I can slip this into?"

"Sure, in the kitchen." Lucia hustled out of the office.

Colleen drummed her fingers on the edge of the desk. "So, Neil, what did you write to your wife?" Assuming the letter was from the chief.

What if the letter was from someone else? Say, Neil's killer? Curiosity ate at her. She wanted to open the letter and see the contents, but doing so could compromise any latent fingerprints.

Lucia returned with a quart-size plastic freezer bag. "Here."

Several other firefighters followed Lucia back to the office and crowded in, their curious and interested expressions mirroring Colleen's feelings. Good. The more witnesses, the better.

With the tip of a pen, she pushed the envelope into the bag and zipped it shut. "I'll take this over to Sam and Becca," she said as she stood.

The firefighters murmured among themselves as they parted to let Colleen and Lucia leave. Lucia walked her friend out to the curb, where Colleen had parked her car.

"You be careful, okay?" Lucia said as she hugged Colleen.

"I will," Colleen assured her.

Stepping back, Lucia nodded. "Don't forget to visit Mary."

"Thanks, Lucia," Colleen said as she opened the door and slid into the driver's seat. She waved at her friend before she drove away.

She glanced at the plastic bag lying on the seat. Once she turned it over to Sam, she'd never see it again. She wasn't ready to give up control of this lead yet.

Instead of driving straight to the police station, she drove to the O'Briens' house, a small, single-level, blue-and-white trimmed home on a tree-lined street. The front yard needed a little attention; the grass was ankle-high and the bushes could stand to be shaped. Obvious signs of a man who'd lost interest in his home and the life he had there. Sadness crept into Colleen's heart.

Colleen pulled into the driveway. Putting the evidence bag with the letter into a big tote, she got out and walked up to the door, then knocked, hoping that Mary would be able to tell her the contents of the letter. Several moments later, Mary O'Brien opened the door.

Colleen's heart twisted. The hugely pregnant widow was obviously suffering. Her red-rimmed eyes and pink nose gave testament to her sorrow. Neither condemnation nor pleasure at seeing Colleen showed in her pretty face, only grief.

Wiping her nose with a white tissue, Mary cocked her head. "What can I do for you?"

"I'm hoping you can answer a few questions for me, Mary," Colleen replied gently.

"I've told the police all I know," she said, sniffing.

Colleen pulled out the letter from her bag. "Do you know anything about this?"

Mary's eyes grew round. She grabbed Colleen's arm and dragged her inside. "Where did you find that?"

"Hidden in your husband's desk. Is the letter from him?"

Mary shook her head. "No. I don't know who it's from." She stared at the zippered plastic bag with loathing.

"Can you tell me the contents?" Colleen gently probed.

Mary waved her hand dismissively. "You can open it."

Colleen shook her head. "It's evidence." She didn't want her fingerprints on it at all.

Mary sat on the worn brown sofa. "Neil was a good man. He tried real hard to be a good husband and I know he wanted to be a good father."

Colleen thought back over Neil's behavior the last few months. His antagonism toward Lucia and his aggressiveness in trying to have her kicked out of the firehouse didn't coincide with the picture Mary was painting.

"What happened?" Colleen asked as she sat on the ottoman a few paces away. Sometimes she learned the most when she just allowed people to tell their story in their own way.

"We tried for a baby for eight long years. The doctors told us to be patient. We tried. All the tests and fertility drugs cost money. The insurance picked up some, but we were struggling. I think Neil believed he was doing the right thing by taking what was left of our savings and playing the horses. He won a few times at first, but then…"

The sadness in Mary's eyes spoke volumes about the losses.

"He got in pretty deep. I didn't know how deep

until I received that letter. It has a copy of a promissory note to some bookie in Cripple Creek. We owed way more than we could ever hope to pay back. Neil was so upset when he found out that I'd been sent this letter. He started drinking then."

Colleen thought back to the night of the museum gala. Neil had definitely been intoxicated that night.

"How long ago did you receive this?" Colleen asked.

Mary shrugged. "A few months back. I told Sam and Becca about his gambling and they said they'd look into it."

"Do you remember the name of the man in Cripple Creek?"

"Hank...something, at the Tree Top Tavern."

It was a lead. A place to start. Colleen took Mary's hand. "I hope you realize I didn't have anything to do with Neil's death."

Fresh tears spilled down Mary's plump cheeks. "I know, Colleen. I never once thought you could have done this, no matter what anybody said. I think whoever killed my husband was the one who called me."

Colleen stilled. "Called you?"

Mary nodded. "A few months before the letter arrived, I received a strange call. The voice was deep, gravelly, telling me to tell Neil that if he didn't do as planned he could forget about ever seeing his child." She shuddered.

"I never told Neil about it because I was afraid of how he'd react. I worried about his health. Instead, I told your cousin Brendan. He said he'd look into it without involving the police. I don't know if he ever found anything." She shrugged. "I'm sure it was probably the man Neil owed so much money to."

Her mind running through the possible scenarios, Colleen agreed. A loan shark. A mob boss. The casinos. Any number of unscrupulous people could have been involved. "Probably. I know the authorities will uncover the truth."

Mary sighed. "Now, if you don't mind, I'd like to take a nap. I just don't have much strength these days."

Colleen stood, mentally making a note to ask her mother, Liza, to check in on Mary. "Thank you for your time. If you need anything, please let me know."

Mary pushed herself from the couch and walked Colleen to the door. "Be careful, Colleen."

"I will. You, too," Colleen said as she walked away. The door closed quietly behind her.

In her car, Colleen sat and contemplated her next move. Sam would be *very* angry if she didn't get the envelope to him soon. But following this lead was important.

Her brothers would skin her alive if she took off

to Cripple Creek alone. She thought about calling Lucia and asking her to go with her, but Lucia had her own job and life to contend with. Colleen could call Jake or Adam or even Brendan. Only she had no doubt they'd take the information and head off without her.

She had to do this alone. She pushed aside the unbidden image of a dark-haired, handsome man who'd been there to help her once before.

Driving away from town, Colleen glanced in her rearview mirror and noticed a familiar red sports car trailing along behind her. Her pulse kicked up a beat. No way!

Alessandro.

Why was he following her? Did he think he'd have to bail her out of trouble again? It was one thing for her to think about needing him and another for him to assume she needed him.

She turned into the parking lot of a convenience store. The little red sports car pulled up alongside her and Alessandro emerged from the car. His white linen pants were creased from sitting and his tab-collar shirt made him look as if he should be standing on the bow of a yacht instead of in the Quick Stop parking lot.

Her heart thumped. He sure was handsome. Colleen rolled down her window. "Are you following me?"

His mouth quirked on one side. "You could say that, *bella.*"

She tried to stop the little flutter of excitement in the pit of her stomach. She should be angry. "I will say it. And I want to know why."

He shrugged, the quintessential Italian male gesture. "You are not one to sit idle while some person is out there framing you for murder."

Her chin dipped at the praise in his tone. Most people saw her assertive independence as a negative. "You think you know me pretty well, don't you?"

His shoulders rose in another careless shrug and an amused glint entered his eyes. "It wouldn't take, what is that saying?…a brain surgeon to figure you out."

A dry laugh escaped. "I'm that transparent?"

His grin flashed briefly, dazzling against his olive skin. "I'd rather say you're a dedicated professional."

Another compliment. Wow!

"Good recovery." She studied him for a moment. He was big, strong, capable of protecting her if she should need it. She wouldn't score any points with her family, but hey, at least she wouldn't be alone. And that was the only reason she'd ever admit to for wanting him with her. Regardless of the torture device. "Would you be willing to do me a huge favor?"

He blinked. "Again?"

She had the grace to blush at the reminder of how

she'd used him to escape her brothers at the police station. But she also remembered that he hadn't answered her questions about his daughter.

In fact, he'd been rather upset with her. But this was another day and another opportunity to gather information. Not only on O'Brien, but on Alessandro.

"I'm checking out a lead on Neil O'Brien's gambling. Would you want to tag along with me to Cripple Creek?"

He cocked his head. "Tag along?"

She grinned. "Come with me."

"Ah." He rubbed his chin for a moment. "Only if I drive."

She eyed the red sports car. "If we can put the top down."

He laughed, a rich, mellow sound that warmed her to her toes. "*Sì, bella.* Anything you wish."

Talk about a loaded statement. There was much she wished but was too afraid to voice regarding the handsome man standing beside her. Keeping an emotional distance was paramount to success in investigative journalism.

Grabbing her tote, she locked up her car and climbed into his passenger seat. Alessandro slid behind the wheel.

"So tell me, *cara.* Why are we going to Cripple Creek?" he asked as he pulled the car back onto the highway.

"I found out that O'Brien was up to his eyeballs in debt and the debt was being called in. I want to see what the man who Neil did business with has to say."

Alessandro frowned. "Shouldn't you let the police handle such things?"

Guilt pinched her conscience but she ignored it. The story came first. "I will hand off my information once I've had a chance to see where this leads."

"Ah, *cara mia*, I worry you put yourself in danger heedlessly."

She touched his arm, his concern for her well-being so sweet and touching. "Well, that's why I invited you along. You're my muscle."

He threw back his head and laughed. She liked his laugh. She settled back and enjoyed the ride, letting the afternoon sun touch her face and the wind breeze by.

She grabbed her ponytail with one hand to keep it from whipping her face to shreds. Alessandro pushed some buttons on the dash and beautiful music filled Colleen's head. An aria from an opera. The men in her life wouldn't know opera from jazz, let alone appreciate it.

The countryside, with lush green aspen trees and crystal-clear streams running through flower-filled meadows, made for a scenic ride. The majestic Rockies tempered the skyline. Colleen craned her neck back to watch what she swore was a bald eagle soaring by. It all was so romantic and…whoa! This isn't some joy ride or a date, she scolded herself.

Very deliberately, she shifted her mind back onto business. She tried once again to broach the subject of his daughter. "What is your child's name?"

His jaw tightened. "*Bella*, let's leave my personal life alone and concentrate on your task."

She wanted to push, but since he was doing her a favor, she decided to let it go for the moment. The car slowed as they entered the restored silver-mining town of Cripple Creek. The squat, brick-front buildings that once housed Old West saloons now housed limited-stakes gambling casinos. The exterior of each casino stayed true to the original historic motif, while inside, state-of-the-art gambling machines brought the past into the twenty-first century.

Colleen and Alessandro climbed out of the car and headed into the small casino called Tree Top Tavern. The acrid scent of tobacco smoke clogged Colleen's senses. She coughed and blinked at the stinging in her eyes. There was something about gambling that drew smokers and drinkers.

Colleen knew from her previous research on the rise of drugs that gambling, smoking and drinking were part and parcel of the obsessive and addictive personality traits common to those whose lives were brought down by such things. Sad, really. But a choice made.

Colleen headed straight to the bar. A burly man with thinning steel gray hair, beady green eyes and a scraggly beard grunted a greeting.

"Excuse me, can you tell me where I'd find Hank?"

The man narrowed his eyes, making them almost disappear in the fleshy folds of his face. His gaze shifted from Colleen to Alessandro, who stood behind her. "What you want Hank for?"

Colleen offered her most nonthreatening smile. "I just have some questions."

The burly man jerked his head at Alessandro. "You two cops?"

Colleen shook her head. "No. I'm a reporter for the *Colorado Springs Sentinel*. Really, I just have some questions. Nothing big."

Regarding them warily, the man said, "Wait here."

He walked to the end of the bar and spoke to a thin, dark-haired man, who turned to stare at them. His ebony eyes assessed them for a moment, then he nodded, got up and walked to a curtained doorway. He motioned for Colleen and Alessandro to follow with a flick of his hand.

Anticipation raced along Colleen's veins as she moved to follow. Trailing their guide through a small, square storage area and down a long, dimly lit hall, apprehension closed in and she was thankful she'd asked Alessandro to accompany her. Funny how she felt so secure with him around.

At the end of the hall the thin man held up his hand to halt them. He knocked on a door. A moment later the door opened and a broad-shouldered behemoth came out and patted them down for weapons. This wasn't the first time she'd been searched by a thug. Nor did she suppose it would be the last.

They were then escorted inside.

Colleen found herself face-to-face with a weaselly-looking man sitting at a large desk. Piles of papers were stacked around. An aura of filth made Colleen's skin tighten. Alessandro placed a hand on her shoulder, his palm warm and comforting. She glanced at him and he inclined his head slightly as if to say, "Ask your questions."

She cleared her throat. "Are you Hank?"

"I am." He pointed a finger. "What does a reporter from the *Sentinel* want with me?"

"Do you remember taking some promissory notes from Neil O'Brien?"

His eyes narrowed to suspicious slits. "Yeah."

"Were you pressuring him to pay back his loans?"

Hank sat back and shook his head. "Nope. His loans were paid off a while ago. I haven't seen O'Brien for a long time."

Colleen frowned. "He paid his notes off?"

A wicked smile stretched Hank's lips. "*He* didn't pay them off."

Her pulse jumped. "Who did?"

"What's it worth to you?"

"I—"

Alessandro cut Colleen off. "That's the wrong question."

She turned to look at him. The fierce light in his dark eyes took her by surprise.

Hank raised an insolent brow. "Oh. And what is the right one?"

"The question should be, what happens if you don't cooperate?"

Colleen shuddered. Alessandro had issued a challenge that surely he realized was ridiculous. He couldn't make Hank talk. Not when there were two mean-looking men standing by who'd no doubt be quite capable of hurting both of them. Fear slammed a fist into her midsection. She'd brought them into this situation. She'd put Alessandro in danger.

Alessandro held Hank's gaze. He must have communicated some silent threat because finally Hank shifted his gaze away and shrugged. "Makes no never mind to me. Some swanky couple came in and bought the notes."

"Swanky?" Colleen asked.

"Yeah. Kinda like you two, only more so. The

lady dripped diamonds and the guy was a real metro type. You know, dressed real nice and looking down his nose. Only he wasn't so tall."

"Can you describe them? Hair color, eye color?"

"Look, lady, I didn't study them. They paid cash, I gave them the notes and that was that. I ain't seen them since. Now, if you're done, I've got work to do."

Alessandro put his hand on Colleen's elbow and guided her out of the casino. Once they were back on the road, Colleen asked, "Do you believe him?"

Alessandro looked thoughtful. "Yes. I do."

"Why? The guy's a sleazeball."

Alessandro's mouth quirked. "The guy's too *stupido* to make up a good lie."

"I guess. I wonder who the couple he was talking about could be. Who would buy the notes and then send a copy to Mary?"

"I think you need to put all this in Sam's hands."

She pulled a face. "Yeah, I know I need to."

They drove back to Colorado Springs in silence. Colleen mulled over what they'd learned. She didn't get it. None of the clues added up. Another cryptic dead end for her story. Maybe Sam could put the pieces together.

Alessandro pulled his car next to hers in the Quick Stop parking lot. He got out and came around the car to open her door. She took his outstretched hand, liking the way her smaller one fit nicely against his palm. She couldn't deny they fit well together as a team.

He raised her hand and briefly kissed the back, sending delighted little chills racing over her senses.

"You'll go straight to Sam?" he asked, his compelling gaze intense.

"Yes." She forced her mind to function. "Thank you for me taking out there."

"My pleasure, *bella.*"

He helped her into her car and then strode back to his own. She watched him drive away. She really liked him, even if he remained a mystery to her. Even if she'd sworn she'd never take a chance on a romantic relationship. Not that she was now, only... She sighed. It felt nice to be treated so sweetly.

She shook off the silly notion and drove to the police station. Sam wasn't at his desk. She plopped down on his vacant cloth-covered chair. On the top of the desk was a file folder with Neil O'Brien's name on the tab.

Everything inside her itched to open the file and read the information on the investigation. She glanced around as her hand rested on the top of the file, her nails playing with the edge.

"I sure hope you don't plan to peek in that."

Sam's voice came from her right. She jerked her hand away and flushed hotly. "No. Well...maybe I was thinking about it. Can you blame me?"

Sam, looking haggard in wrinkled clothes and

with dark circles under his eyes, motioned for her to get out of his chair. She complied and dragged over a metal chair.

"No, I don't blame you, but it would look really bad if there was even a hint that you influenced the investigation, Colleen."

Wincing, she put her hand on her tote. "Uh, well. I hope this won't come across as tampering with evidence, but…" She pulled out the zippered plastic bag. "Here."

Sam took the bag, held it up to examine the contents, then turned hard, steely eyes her way. "I'm almost afraid to ask, but where did you get this?"

"Neil's office."

Sam groaned. "Colleen, you shouldn't have gone there. You need to stay as far from this investigation as possible. Deputy Mayor Frost is clamoring for your head on a silver platter."

Colleen blinked. "Oh, man. My father will have a fit if he hears that."

"Yeah, since my dad is still out of commission, Frost is in charge." Sam looked at the bagged envelope again. "Where in his office did you find it? We combed that room."

She told him about the blotter and about visiting Mary O'Brien. She ignored his stern frown, which only deepened when she told him that she'd already checked out Hank in Cripple Creek.

"Woman, you are in so much trouble. What were you thinking? You could have gotten hurt or worse."

She lifted her chin. "I didn't go alone."

"Don't tell me one of your brothers thought this scheme was okay."

"No. I had someone else go with me." *Please, don't let him ask who.*

"Who?"

She ducked her head and mumbled, "Alessandro."

He stared. "Did you just say my cousin's name?"

Taking a deep breath, she met his gaze. "Yes. I asked Alessandro to go with me. See, I'm not a complete ninny."

Through gritted teeth, he said, "I'll deal with my cousin later. What did you learn?"

She frowned and told him about the couple Hank had claimed bought the promissory notes signed by the battalion chief.

Sam ran a hand through his hair. "Interesting. I'll follow up on that. You, on the other hand, are barred from this investigation until you are cleared of all suspicion. Got that? Work on the fires or something else."

She did have something else to concentrate on: the mysterious Alessandro. For her story, most assuredly, but also to figure out the undeniable attraction she felt for the man.

"Okay, Sam. I'll let you do your job, but you'll tell

me if you find out anything more in Cripple Creek and if there are any prints or anything useful from that, right?" She nodded her head to the bag still in his hands.

"Will do."

She stood to leave.

"Colleen."

She looked at her friend and saw the concern in his eyes. "Yes?"

"Be careful."

That was the third time in one day she'd been warned to be careful. She hoped everyone's concern wasn't an indication that trouble was around the corner.

SIX

Alessandro drove to Dahlia's modern high-rise apartment. He was sure Dahlia and Escalante were the couple who had bought the promissory notes from Hank in Cripple Creek. Which meant they had been blackmailing Neil with them. But to what end?

Was Colleen right that Neil had set the fire in the hospital? Had he been ordered to by Escalante? It made no sense. Why would Escalante bother with a hospital fire?

Only Dahlia had the answers. Alessandro would have to continue to pursue her in order to obtain the information he needed to solve the mystery of Neil's death, the fire and the threats to Colleen's life.

His guts contracted with unease at the way Colleen so carelessly put herself in danger. She needed a keeper. Someone to watch her back, since she insisted on continuing her own investigations.

He'd mention it to Sam and pray that would be enough.

* * *

"I don't know if this is such a good idea," Colleen muttered as she climbed out of the back of her parents' dark-green Cadillac. It had been two weeks since Neil's murder, and the coroner had finally released his body for burial. The police still didn't have any other suspects to speak of. Only Colleen, much to her mortification.

"Nonsense." Liza Montgomery linked her arm through her daughter's.

As always, Colleen's mom was dressed immaculately in a classic two-piece suit that fit her plump frame well. Her graying blond hair was stylishly combed back, accentuating her green eyes and rosy cheeks. "You will pay your respects like everyone else."

"Not everyone else is suspected of murdering Neil O'Brien," Colleen shot back as she walked along beside her mother, careful not to step on any graves as they made their way toward the burial site.

"Which galls me to no end," grumbled Frank Montgomery as he fell into step with his family. He adjusted the navy-and-red striped tie at his neck. He looked good in his dark suit, which stretched nicely over his broad shoulders.

Colleen hid a smile as she remembered the way her father had bellowed about the injustice of his only daughter being thought a killer. She'd assured him Sam was only doing his job and that no, Sam didn't have cotton between his ears.

Up ahead, a crowd had gathered on the manicured lawn of the cemetery for the graveside service. As the trio drew closer, Colleen glimpsed the dark wooden coffin resting above a large pit. She shuddered, thinking how dismal it was that some people believed this life ended at the grave, with nothing but darkness beyond.

Thankfully, she had a Savior who would take her soul to Heaven when the time came. She didn't know what Neil's faith had been or even if he'd had any. Sadness brought the day into somber reality.

Her gaze sought out Mary O'Brien, Neil's widow. She sat near the head of the gravesite, flanked on both sides by the men and women of the Colorado Springs Fire Department. The black veil Mary wore hid her face, but Colleen saw her wipe at her tears.

Colleen's heart squeezed with sympathy. "Excuse me," she said and headed across the lawn toward Mary.

As she approached, Mary said, "Colleen, thank you for coming."

Giving the woman a hug, Colleen said, "Let me know if I can do anything for you."

"You're so kind," Mary murmured as she turned to greet someone else.

Colleen took her place beside her parents, joining her brothers and their wives near the middle of the crowd. Colleen's gaze surveyed the faces of those gathered around the grave, wondering if Neil's murderer was among them.

Or had the person responsible not felt enough guilt to attend the funeral of the man whose life had been cut short and whose family had been destroyed?

Who among the people of Colorado Springs had motive to kill Neil? She made eye contact with Sam.

In her heart she knew he didn't believe she'd done this thing, regardless of the fact that he'd found her scarf at the scene of the crime. Anyone could have planted it there. But why? Who had anything to gain by framing her?

Behind her she heard a car pulling up. There were several indrawn breaths as Alessandro Donato stepped out of a limousine.

He looked imposing in a severe black double-breasted suit. Colleen couldn't control the way her heart rate sped up or the vain thought that she was glad she'd worn the dark navy pantsuit that her mother always said flattered her figure. Not that she was hoping Alessandro would notice her figure, but...

Alessandro then turned to help Dahlia Sainsbury out of the car. Colleen's spine stiffened and anger at herself for her foolishness made her teeth ache. Here she was, thankful she was looking good, and he arrived with another woman. Dahlia's black knee-length dress was bettered suited for a cocktail party than a funeral.

The pair joined the funeral service near the back at Colleen's right. Interesting that they'd show up together. More reason to find out the exact nature of their relationship. Purely for her story's sake, of course.

Pastor Gabriel Dawson began the service by reading from the Book of Psalms. Then Ben Kaza, Luke Donovan and Gideon Jackson each took a turn to speak about their chief.

Ben's words were especially touching. He spoke of how Neil had been so encouraging after Ben had lost his sight in a fire earlier in the year. Each man had a tale that spoke of a man Colleen hadn't known. The discrepancy reminded her that humans were very complicated and had many facets.

She glanced over her right shoulder. Her gaze collided with Alessandro's.

Complicated. Yes, definitely.

A man of many facets? She'd find out.

Heat crept into Colleen's cheeks as Alessandro raised an eyebrow as if to ask what she found so interesting. She gave him a tight smile and turned her attention back to the proceedings.

Gideon Jackson informed the crowd that donations for Mary and her unborn child could be made to an account in Mary's name at the local bank. Colleen thought that was such a generous and caring thing for the firefighters to set up.

Pastor Gabriel and his wife Susan led the mourners in singing "Amazing Grace."

A movement at the edge of the cemetery in her direct line of vision snagged her attention. A man stood in the shadow of a large tree, a baseball cap concealing his hair and face.

Colleen sought Sam's attention and motioned with her head toward the tree. Giving her a nod of acknowledgement, he slipped out of the crowd, and to Colleen's astonishment so did Alessandro. But as the two men hurried forward, the man in the shadows fled.

Pastor Gabriel concluded the service with a prayer and then it seemed everyone was talking at once, wondering what had sent Sam running off.

"Hello, all." Lidia Vance came to stand beside the Montgomery clan.

Liza gave her friend a hug. "How's Max?"

"He came home yesterday." Lidia beamed. "He's doing very well. We would love for you all to come to our house later this afternoon for a short homecoming gathering."

"Count us in," Frank said.

Lidia turned to Colleen. "I've talked with Al Crane and we're hoping you'd be interested in writing a piece for the paper on Max and his recovery. Something to let the people of Colorado

Springs know their mayor is still working hard to keep the town safe and in the black."

Colleen blinked. She had two other stories she was working on. Well, three if she counted the mystery of Alessandro Donato. But the expectation in Lidia's eyes, not to mention Liza and Frank Montgomery's, was enough to make her nod. She could multitask.

"Good. We'll see you at the house at three." Lidia moved away to join her daughter, Lucia. Though Lucia had had an antagonistic relationship with Neil O'Brien, Colleen could see the sorrow in her eyes as their gazes met.

Neil had tried to put the blame for the pediatric-wing fire at the hospital on Lucia. No way had Lucia started that fire, either on purpose or accidentally. Lucia was better than that: she was careful and meticulous. No, Neil was responsible for that fire, but with him dead it was going to be a lot harder to prove.

Unless…perhaps he was working for someone and that someone had realized Neil was a threat and had had him killed. Maybe Neil was going to confess his part in the fire. That would explain why someone would off him. But who? The couple who'd bought the gambling debts? She hoped Sam found them soon.

"Are you ready, dear?" asked her mother.

Colleen shook her head as her gaze sought Dahlia.

Why had Neil come to the museum the night of the opening? Was there a connection between Dahlia and Neil? Where did Alessandro fit into the equation?

She spied the woman central to her thoughts standing alone off to the side of the gathering. Colleen quickly scanned the crowd for Alessandro. He was talking with Sam and Becca, probably explaining why he'd gone after the mysterious observer.

She'd have given anything to be privy to that conversation, but instead decided to take the opportunity to have a chat with Dahlia.

"Can you give me another five minutes, Mom?" she asked.

"Of course, dear. Your father and I will be at the car." Liza hooked her arm through her husband's. "Come along, Frank. I'd like to say hi to Joe and Fiona before they leave."

The couple headed toward the cars, where Frank's younger brother, Joe, and his wife were talking with their eldest son, Quinn.

Colleen wasted no time weaving her way through the crowd to Dahlia. "Ms. Sainsbury."

Dahlia's mouth pressed into a tight smile. "Miss Montgomery. Interesting to see you here."

"Yes, well." Colleen ignored the chill in the other woman's voice. "I was hoping I could ask you a few questions."

"If I can answer them, I will," she said pleasantly enough, but her shrewd eyes glittered.

"Do you know why Neil O'Brien showed up at the museum gala?"

"To see the exhibition like everyone else, I suppose," she said with a shrug.

Colleen remembered the way Neil had seemed to be looking for someone. "Had you had any contact with him prior to that night?"

"I didn't have contact with him that night or any other." Dahlia's voice held an edge of irritation.

Interesting. Why would she get defensive?

"How long have you known Alessandro Donato?" Colleen asked, hoping by switching subjects so abruptly, Dahlia might slip her a bit of information. Sometimes the tactic worked and sometimes not.

A calculating gleam entered Dahlia's eyes. "You're interested in Alessandro?"

"Yes. No." Colleen gritted her teeth and fought back the uncomfortable sensation of confusion running through her. "I mean, not in the way your tone implies. I'm interested for purely professional reasons."

"Indeed."

Annoyance flashed at the small smirk on the other woman's face. Okay, this tactic wasn't going the way Colleen had planned. "You didn't answer my question."

Dahlia's gaze shifted beyond Colleen's shoulder,

and without turning around Colleen knew Alessandro was behind her. The air grew thicker and more energized.

And if this strange awareness wasn't happening to her, she'd have scoffed at anyone who'd said such things were possible.

But just to be certain, she turned. Sure enough, there he stood. Mr. Tall, Handsome and Exasperating gave her a slow smile that trapped her breath in her lungs much like a punch to the stomach. A sensation she was familiar with, having grown up with two annoying but loveable brothers.

Any hope of getting information from Dahlia was going to have to wait. Alessandro's warning to stay out of his business and away from Dahlia rang in her head.

Just the sort of thing that intrigued her most. A challenge with a secret.

She would get her information.

Alessandro couldn't stay glued to Dahlia's side forever. Patience would produce an opportunity.

And she'd learn to ignore the uncanny way his presence charged the air around her. Wouldn't she?

"You had a question, Colleen?" Alessandro asked, his gaze steady on the blonde before him.

What he really wanted to do was shake her and ask why she wasn't staying away from Dahlia Sainsbury as he'd warned her to do. Someday her nosy nature was going to land her in trouble. His gut twisted. Falcon had said not to worry about her anymore, but that was proving impossible.

Colleen's cute mouth tightened and frustration radiated from her blue eyes. "Alessandro. Did you catch the man you and Sam went after?"

"Nothing escapes you, does it, *bella?*"

Her chin lifted. "No, it doesn't."

In other words, she wasn't going to give up digging into his life, and she definitely wasn't going to stay away from Dahlia. Admiring her tenacity but deploring her stubbornness, Alessandro ground his back teeth. "I'm sure Sam can fill you in. Ms. Sainsbury and I were just leaving. Can we give you a lift somewhere?"

Colleen's gaze darted between him and Dahlia. "No, I wouldn't want to intrude." She turned her back to him. "Ms. Sainsbury, I hope that we can continue this conversation another time?"

"Perhaps," Dahlia intoned with a slight incline of her head.

"Yes, well." Colleen backed away. "Goodbye." She turned and hurried to where her parents waited at their big luxury car.

"She's got it bad for you."

Dahlia's amused tone scraped across his nerves. Alessandro shook his head. "No. She's just after a story."

"Is she going to find one?"

"Not if I can help it." He gave her a sly, conspiratorial smile before offering her his arm. "Shall we?"

Dahlia placed her cool fingers on his arm. He forced Colleen out of his mind and turned his concentration to Dahlia. He hoped if she believed he could present her with a profitable opportunity, she would begin to let down her guard.

He had to find Escalante soon. He didn't know how much longer he had until either Colleen outed him or he was officially pulled from the case. Either way, he would succeed.

Failure was not an option.

Colleen arrived at the Vance family home at exactly three o'clock. She hadn't changed out of her navy tailored pantsuit, since she was making this visit in a professional capacity to interview the mayor. She hated this weakness in herself that wanted to seek everyone's approval, but here she was and she'd do her best. As always.

She parked her compact sedan on the street and walked up the cobbled walkway to the front door. The grand Victorian home graced Canyon Drive, located on the west side of town, like a beautiful painted lady.

Triangular gables, a tower that peeked over the roof from the back of the house and the stunning wraparound front porch made one think of stepping into a different era. Passersby on the street could see the delicate lacy curtains adorning the large front bay window.

She'd recognized several cars as she'd driven up. Her parents', Sam's, Michael Vance's truck, Lucia's go-cart, as Colleen affectionately called her friend's little two-door. And Alessandro's red convertible parked alongside Travis Vance's rig. A good old family gathering.

She wondered how the Vances got along with their cousin from Lidia's side of the family, aside from suspecting that Alessandro had something to do with Max's shooting.

Obviously, if they really thought he had been involved, they wouldn't allow him in the house. Did they know about his hero complex? If nothing else, his presence affirmed her instincts that he wasn't what he seemed.

She rang the bell, and a moment later the door was swung open by Peter Vance. Tall, with blue-black hair and killer blue eyes, Peter was the kind of man who made you feel comfortable with his easy smile.

She could see how Dr. Emily Armstrong had fallen twice for her husband, but Colleen wondered how Emily coped with the risk of losing Peter, not through normal marital problems but through

Peter's work at AdVance. A P.I. still took a chance when working.

"Hey, Colleen, come on in," Peter said.

"How's it going, Peter?" she asked as she stepped across the threshold.

"Great. Emily's working at the hospital today but Manuel is here, running around like a wild horse."

From down the hall, she heard the distinct sound of a pretend whinny. "Literally, I take it."

Peter grinned, the obvious love for his adopted son glowing in his eyes. "I've got kid duty. Manuel and Sam's trio are all in the family room. Everyone else is upstairs visiting. Go on up."

"Thanks, Peter," Colleen said as she made her way up the impressive wide staircase.

She loved the homey, old-fashioned feel that Lidia and Max had created with striking antiques and family heirlooms. At the top of the stairs she followed the sound of voices coming from the last room on her right. She knocked softly and was admitted by Lucia, who squeezed her tightly in a warm embrace.

Colleen's gaze swept the room and landed on Alessandro. He'd changed out of his dark suit and into pressed khakis and a striped button-down shirt that molded nicely to his tall form. He leaned against the wall a bit away from the rest as if he were merely an observer.

Something sad shifted in Colleen.

It must be so lonesome to be a part of a family yet not. But he did have a family of his own. At least a child.

Did the Vances know about Alessandro's off-spring? Or was he keeping her a secret from them as well? Now was not an appropriate time to ask, but she would eventually, after she had more information on Alessandro.

She began to turn away, but Alessandro's dark gaze met hers. She started to form a smile but stalled. There was something odd in the way he looked at her. A reserved, polite detachment that hadn't been there before.

As if the conversations and the flirting they'd shared had never happened.

Just two acquaintances in the same room.

Was that because his relationship with Dahlia was growing deeper? All the more reason to question the museum curator for the answers she sought.

Lidia waved Colleen in from her place beside her husband's bed. Puzzling over the lack of…sparks… from Alessandro, for want of a better word, she moved forward with nods and murmurs of greetings to the others in the room. Mayor Vance lay on a hos-pital-style bed, still hooked up to monitors, but his color looked better than the last time she'd seen him a few weeks ago.

He smiled and held out his hand. "Lidia tells me you agreed to write up a blurb for the paper."

His hand felt comfortably warm to her touch. "Yes, sir."

"Good. Basically, we need the people of Colorado Springs to know I'm recovering, that I'm in my right mind and the doctors say I should be back to good health before too long. I want to thank everyone for their prayers and the overwhelming love and support the town has given to my family and me."

"Consider it done, Your Honor."

Max squeezed her hand. "Now, while the time of this gathering has proven unfortunate because of what happened to Neil, I still think we should have a toast."

Colleen looked to Lidia with surprise, but smiled as bottles of sparkling apple cider were served.

Sam held up his glass. "To my father. May God bless your recovery and bless this family."

"Hear, hear," agreed the others as they took sips of the bubbling juice.

Colleen moved around the room chatting, but her mind and gaze kept straying to Alessandro. What had changed between them?

She shrugged off the question and realized this would be a perfect opportunity to head over to the museum to talk with Dahlia, since Alessandro was now engrossed in a conversation with Travis and Sam.

She said some quick goodbyes, though Lidia

seemed the most reluctant to let her go. Colleen promised she would bring an advance copy of her article for their approval.

Colleen managed to leave relatively quickly and headed as fast as the speed limit allowed across town to the museum. She parked on a side street where she had a clear view of the entrance so if Dahlia wasn't there, Colleen would be able to see her arrive.

The guard at the door assured Colleen that Ms. Sainsbury was in her office. Colleen walked through the museum, now fairly empty and quiet as opposed to the night of the gala. A movement in her peripheral vision stopped her cold.

She glimpsed the retreating back of a man with a familiar cut to his shoulders as he entered another section of the museum. Alessandro? Colleen scoffed.

Alessandro wasn't here. He couldn't be. He was still at the mayor's house. She shrugged off the insane thought that she was seeing him around every corner.

Really, she didn't have a thing for the man; it was just that his undiscovered story was percolating in her brain.

At the door marked Curator, she knocked. Dahlia's voice held a note of frustration as she said, "Enter."

Colleen stepped into the office. The Spartan space

was a study in shades of cream and made a striking backdrop to the woman in charge. A colorful Persian rug graced the floor and a beautifully preserved sideboard resided against the far wall.

Dahlia had changed out of the black dress she'd worn to the funeral into a vivid yellow flowing two-piece suit that accentuated her elegant frame and made her pale complexion glow. Her dark hair was in its traditional twist, but long black sticks with gold scrolling on them pierced it.

"I told you I'd be a minute, Mr.—" Dahlia arched an eyebrow as she looked up. Clearly she'd been expecting someone else. "What can I do for you, Miss Montgomery?"

"I'd like to continue our conversation from this morning." Colleen walked farther into the room, determined not to be put off.

"I'm very busy and I have meetings scheduled." Dahlia shuffled the papers on the desk into a pile and shoved them in a drawer.

"This won't take long, I promise."

Dahlia sighed and relaxed into the high-backed leather chair. "Please, have a seat." She indicated the stiff, no-frills chair opposite the desk.

Colleen obediently sat. Obviously the chair was designed so the occupant wouldn't want to stay for long. "I'll get right to the point. What is your connection to Alessandro Donato?"

"Business. What is your interest in him?"

"Professional. I'm doing a piece on newcomers to our town and he's a fascinating subject."

Dahlia's painted lips curved upward. "Indeed. I told him you had a thing for him, but he didn't believe me. You do have a thing for him, don't you?"

Colleen pursed her lips. Her immediate instinct was to give a resounding no! Yet that wasn't the complete truth. *Thing* was too strong a word, and had the wrong connotation.

But if it would help her get the story, she could play up her interest in Alessandro. "There are rumors that he's a bit of a playboy, but I haven't seen much evidence of that, other than his close association with you. Are you romantically involved with him?"

Dahlia steepled her fingers and clicked her French-manicured nails together. A beautiful diamond tennis bracelet twinkled in the muted light. "I can assure you I am not."

Colleen didn't detect any guile in Dahlia's response.

Relief at that news caught Colleen by surprise, but only because she couldn't envision such a passionate man with such a cold woman. Yet…she remembered the remoteness in his eyes earlier. He seemed to have two sides. "What can you tell me about him?"

A knowing look entered Dahlia's gaze. "Beyond

that he's extraordinarily handsome, charming and, as far as I know, extremely available? Nothing."

"He can't be too available if he has a child," Colleen muttered, wondering how he could be so blithely going about his business here in the United States when he had a little girl waiting for him in Italy. And where was the child's mother?

Dahlia straightened and leaned forward. "What did you say?"

"Uh, well…" Colleen tried to backpedal as she realized she'd spoken her thought out loud. "Where did you grow up as a child?"

Dahlia narrowed her eyes. "You said he has a child." She sat back and tapped her lips with the end of her index finger. "Very interesting."

Uh-oh. Colleen's stomach knotted up as the implications of what she'd just done swamped her. She'd revealed unconfirmed information to an outside source who could jeopardize her story.

But more importantly, something inside warned her that the information could somehow jeopardize Alessandro.

Stop your probing before someone gets hurt.

When would she learn to keep her mouth shut?

SEVEN

Determined to change the topic from Alessandro's personal life, Colleen asked, "You said you hadn't met Neil O'Brien, but he must have had an invitation or he wouldn't have been let in. Did you personally oversee the guest list for the gala?"

Dahlia's expression stiffened. "I had my administrative assistant make up the list since she's more familiar with the residents of Colorado Springs."

Interesting how Dahlia's manner became aloof except when the subject was Alessandro. She obviously had a "thing" for him as well. A competitive possessiveness seized Colleen by surprise. She ignored it and stayed on task. "Could I speak with your assistant?" Colleen asked.

"You could, if she were here. She left on vacation the day after the gala. She won't be back for another week."

Convenient. "Did she hire the wait staff as well?"

Dahlia nodded. "I don't trouble myself with such tasks."

Of course not, Colleen thought uncharitably. You wouldn't want to break a nail or snag your hose. Colleen mentally chided herself for her uncharacteristic cattiness. She couldn't fathom why Dahlia bugged her so much.

"You do have the name of the company that supplied the staff?" Colleen asked, trying to keep impatience from tingeing her voice.

"Yes. I gave all the information I had to the police. Maybe you should check with them since they probably have more time for this than I do." Dahlia imperiously rose from the chair.

Colleen stood, but wasn't about to be stopped that easily. "One last question. Do you know how my blue scarf got from the coat room to the crime scene?"

Dahlia rounded the desk, her immaculately made-up face expressionless. "No," she responded curtly. "I suggest you ask the police. I assume they talked with the girl whose responsibility it was to monitor the coats and wraps."

Colleen had asked the police, but had been stonewalled. Sam had said he couldn't give her anything pertaining to an ongoing investigation. Which wasn't an absolute, because he had in the past. Only this time was different.

She was considered a "person of interest."

Hurt and anger warred whenever she thought about Sam and Becca even considering she'd had anything to do with Neil's death. So much for loyalty.

Okay, that wasn't fair. They were doing their jobs. But it still didn't make the sting any more comfortable.

She'd have to work with what she could discover on her own.

So, if Dahlia hadn't known Neil, then who could he have been looking for that night? The couple? "Do you keep records of contributors to the museum?"

That would at least give her some names to start looking into.

Dahlia opened the door. "I respect the privacy of our contributors." The phone on her desk rang and she picked up the receiver. "Now, if you'll excuse me." She waved a hand in dismissal.

"Thank you for your time." Colleen walked out and the door clicked shut behind her. She stopped and put her ear to the door. She heard Dahlia say in a forceful voice that she'd be right there.

Curious as always, Colleen decided she'd follow Dahlia and see if she could learn anything useful for her story. Make that *stories*.

Colleen moved to crouch behind a partition that didn't reach the ceiling and waited. A moment later footsteps sounded on the hardwood floor. She peeked around the corner and saw Alessandro Donato approach Dahlia's office. Her pulse shot up. She'd managed to go a handful of minutes without thinking about him, and in he walked.

Odd that he'd changed back into the black well-cut suit he'd worn to the funeral. And now he carried a briefcase. He knocked lightly and then disappeared inside.

Setting her jaw with absurd annoyance, Colleen folded her arms over her chest as she stood. This was an interesting development. Maybe their relationship was strictly business?

She moved to the door again and put her ear once more against the wood. She could hear the low mumble of voices but this time couldn't make out the words.

"Um, excuse me," said a male voice.

Colleen jerked around to find a gray-haired guard giving her a stern look. She smiled sheepishly and hurried out of the museum.

Once in her car, she rethought her plan and decided that she'd follow Alessandro when he came out.

She settled back to wait and tried not to think about what was going on in that office.

Or why she cared.

"My buyer would like written confirmation that you'll procure the piece in question within a reasonable amount of time, for the agreed-upon price," Alessandro stated smoothly, wondering how Dahlia intended to produce the Caravaggio in question when he knew good and well it was locked up tight in the Louvre.

Dahlia fidgeted with the diamond bracelet on her wrist. "Paper can leave a trail. You'll have to trust me. I'll have the painting here by next week. You just make sure the money is in the account I've provided by then."

"Trust is such a complicated issue, do you not think so?" She eyed him, clearly suspicious of his meaning. He obliged by adding. "I would trust you more if you told me how you plan to retrieve the painting."

Her lips thinned. "I have my ways. A greased palm here and there can accomplish much."

Including killing innocent people. A low burn started in his belly. She, along with Escalante, would be brought to justice. He'd see to that.

Casually, stretching out his legs in the uncomfortable little chair, he asked, "Where does your cash flow come from?"

A shrewdness darkened her eyes. "Art can be very lucrative."

"Art only? Or do you have other investments that might be interesting to a man like me with connections in Europe and Asia?" The question was a gamble, one he hoped would pay off if she let slip some information useful in his quest to find Escalante.

Her eyes narrowed. "You ask a lot of questions. Let's see how this deal goes before we look much further into the future." She rose from behind her desk. "I'm sorry to cut this meeting short, but the museum is closing. I have a dinner engagement and don't wish to be late. You know how that is."

Rising also, he nodded. "Yes, of course. I won't keep you."

Opening a large drawer in the wall cabinet behind her, she pulled out a small purse. Alessandro glimpsed a stack of books, the size of journals and ledgers, before she slid the drawer shut and locked it with a small gold key that she then slipped into her purse. He might have to take a peek in that drawer later.

He opened the office door for her, which she locked behind them, and then he followed her through the museum to the service entrance. There she said good-night to the guard and preceded Alessandro out the door.

They were halfway to the corner of the parking lot when he stopped and made a dramatic show of gesturing with his hand. *"Io idiot!"*

"Excuse me?" Dahlia glared at him.

"No, no. *Scusi* me." He put his hand on his chest in a humble posture. "I was so caught up in our conversation that I left my briefcase in your office."

She lifted a shoulder. "You can retrieve it tomorrow."

"No, *signorina*. I need my case tonight. My work is in there and I must send in my report. You do understand the importance of such need?"

She frowned and suspicion lurked in her gaze. "You wait here. I'll go get it."

"Ah, you have saved my life," he stated and followed her back to the service door.

She threw him a frown as she dug a white access card out of her purse and swiped it through the magnetic pad. Then she turned her back to him. But he towered high enough above her that he had a clear view of the number code she punched into the key pad. Committing the sequence to memory, he followed her in.

The guard had begun securing the museum for the night. Instead of the flat-white glow pouring down from overhead, a subtle light emitted from the baseboards cast eerie shadows on the floor.

Most modern galleries used red low-level lights at night, placed advantageously to allow staff members to pass through while keeping the paintings in comparative darkness to reduce the fading effects of overexposure to light.

"Hurry up. The system will rearm the doors in five minutes if I don't reset it from my office."

Noticing a panel in the wall, he asked, "Can't you reset it from here?"

"I could, but I'd rather we do this quickly."

He inclined his head. "Of course."

The guard was nowhere in sight as they walked back to her office. Alessandro glanced at the camera monitors in the corners, which he knew were used more as deterrents than as security devices. She unlocked the door and stepped aside. His briefcase sat on the floor beside the chair. As he passed through the doorway, he brushed his hand across the trunk latch, leaving behind a clear film that would allow the latch to close but not lock.

Picking up the case, he nodded to Dahlia. *"Grazie."*

"Right. Come on. I'm getting later by the second."

As he passed her through the open doorway, he purposely stumbled against her. In a quick sleight of hand, he confiscated the white access card from her open purse.

She pushed him away and snapped, "Are you always such a klutz?"

"Only around beautiful women," he responded smoothly, hoping to stall her long enough to force her to reset the alarm so he could have that code as well.

With a roll of her dark eyes, she pulled the door shut. Using a silver key hanging on a gold keychain, she locked the door. And then with heels clicking rapidly across the hardwood floor, she moved to the service door.

In silence, they walked to the parking lot. He took

her hands and lightly kissed her knuckles, the flesh icy to his touch. "Until tomorrow then, Dahlia."

The assessing look in her eyes tripped his instincts. Had she guessed his true motives for pursuing her? Did she realize he'd lifted the card from her possession?

It wouldn't be long before she found the card missing. His time frame narrowed by a notch. He had to find some answers *now,* while he had the opportunity.

He gave her a lazy, charming smile that usually produced the results he wanted from females. If anything, her expression became colder rather than warmer as he'd hoped.

"Yes, until tomorrow," she said as she slipped into her sedan. A moment later the expensive car roared to life and eased away from the curb to join the afternoon traffic heading through town.

Alessandro waited until she was no longer in sight before he made a grand show of walking away from the museum. An odd prickling at the back of his neck made him cautious.

Someone was watching. He couldn't pinpoint the threat's location. Nothing suspicious caught his eye on the block or the side streets.

He couldn't worry about it now. He had to get into the museum and back out before Dahlia discovered her card missing and came looking for it. He hoped she'd assume she'd lost it somewhere between the museum and her car. Even if she suspected he'd taken it, she'd have no proof unless he was caught.

Inside his briefcase he held the schematics of the museum, but they wouldn't tell him anything he didn't already know. The outer doors were the only worry at the moment as long as he didn't try to take a painting from the wall, which would activate the newest trend in museum security—containment.

If a thief disturbed a piece of artwork, the alarm system would set in motion the new type of security in which a large iron gate would drop from the ceiling, effectively trapping the intruder inside. It was much easier to keep a villain in than out.

Alessandro just needed to make it from the door to Dahlia's office before the guard started asking questions.

And the only way that would happen was if it appeared as if Dahlia had returned.

Colleen sat hunkered down behind the wheel of her car, watching as Alessandro and Dahlia left the museum for the second time and headed to a silver BMW. It figured the uppity British curator would drive a sleek foreign car.

Colleen didn't trust that woman and she didn't trust the association between Dahlia and Alessandro.

On the night of the museum gala, Alessandro had mentioned a buyer for an art piece. Why would an accountant act as art broker? That was a question that had bugged her since that night.

She started the car as Alessandro briskly walked down the street, but then she quickly turned off the engine and slid down so she could peer over the steering wheel. Alessandro had stopped and now faced the window of a store. She'd seen Sam do that once when he'd thought they were being followed.

Colleen dared to rise up a bit more to see if there was anyone else around. No pedestrians, only the occasional car driving by. After hours on Fourth Street seemed pretty quiet.

Colleen watched with interest as Alessandro doubled back and then stepped behind a large bush. What *was* he doing?

A moment later, a tall figure emerged from behind the bush. Colleen's jaw dropped.

Alessandro had on a long black wig and an ankle-length dark trench coat.

She started to chuckle in disbelief. "Oh, my word, what…?"

Was he trying to look like Dahlia?

He approached the museum with a card in his hand, swiped it through the black box next to the service door and deftly used the keypad. Then he disappeared into the museum.

Mind reeling, Colleen scrambled out of the car and ran across the street. She tried the door, but it was locked. She had to get in there and see what Alessandro was up to.

Dressed as a woman? Was he insane? No one could mistake him for a female.

The thought briefly crossed her mind that she should call Sam and Becca and tell them that Alessandro had just sneaked into the museum, but she dismissed the idea. This was her story, her scoop. Her editor's promise of a raise notwithstanding, she loved a juicy challenge. Took giddy pleasure in tracking down the truth. She wasn't about to let this opportunity to reveal Alessandro's strange actions pass her by.

She rejected the little whisper that taunted that in finding out before the police she could somehow protect Alessandro. He hardly needed protection. And if he were up to no good, he deserved whatever the resulting consequences were.

But she couldn't forget what Alessandro had done for Holly and Jake.

He'd saved their lives. Why?

Was Alessandro good or bad?

Every instinct screamed *good.* She could only hope so and refused to consider why it was so important to her.

She hurried around to the back of the historic building, hoping that in the renovations the secret entrance hadn't been discovered and destroyed. As a child, she and her brothers had played in the old structure on many occasions, pretending they were knights or royalty and this was their fortress.

She pushed her way through the bushes, catching her suit on the branches. In the renovations a protruding facade had been added to the outside of the building. Squeezing between the two structures, she searched for the entrance.

Ah, success. There at the base of the wall was the outline of a window. Just the right size for three preteen kids to squeeze through.

She prayed she'd fit through now. Kneeling down, in an awkward position, she ran her fingers around the bottom until she found the latch. She hesitated. What if the window had security sensors?

Deciding the risk was worth taking, she flipped the latch up and pulled. The rusty hinges groaned and moved with agonizing slowness as she raised the pane.

Heart pounding in anxious anticipation, she waited several minutes, expecting to hear sirens or some commotion indicating the security system had been breached.

She peered inside the shadowed room. No sign of any guard. Or anything else, for that matter. The room apparently was unused or maybe even forgotten.

Her heart slowed somewhat as she concluded that this particular window hadn't been wired with an alarm. Maybe they figured no one could get through such a tiny hole, let alone take a valuable painting out of the opening.

The latter part she'd agree with, but... She maneuvered herself feet first through the gap, squirming and wincing as the dull edges scraped her hips and shoulders, bruising her skin and ruining her suit. She landed on the wooden floor of the old, dormant boiler room.

The musty scent of rust and earth tickled her nose. The big mechanical beast that used to scare her years ago she barely noticed now.

A terrifying thought assailed her as she hurried through the cobwebs to the door on the other side of the small space. What if she was now trapped in the boiler room?

One quick glance around chilled her bones. There used to be crates that she and her brothers would stack up like ladders in order to reach the window. The crates were gone. Acutely aware that she'd have no way of reaching the window, she fought off panic.

Taking a deep breath, she turned the knob of the door and pulled. With a squeak that echoed inside her head like the loud clang of a cymbal, the door moved. Heart racing, she waited for the din of an alarm or the sound of the guard's running feet as he came to investigate the noise.

Nothing happened.

She breathed a soft sigh of relief, but moved cautiously out of the boiler room and down a long, narrow hall into the basement of the museum.

Splashes of color bombarded her, tightening her chest and constricting her breathing. The newly renovated basement now served as a storage area.

Paintings of varying sizes and styles covered every available bit of space. A staircase leading up into the museum was on her right. In the wall opposite the old boiler room was another door.

But what sent disappointment spiraling through her was the man standing in the middle of the room, putting paintings into a canvas bag.

She broke the silence of the room. "I can't believe it."

How could she have been so wrong about him?

EIGHT

Alessandro hated seeing the accusation and scorn in Colleen's bright blue eyes. His heart twisted in agony knowing what she thought she'd found him doing. But to tell her he was recovering paintings that had been stolen from other collections and museums in Europe and in the States would blow his cover. Better to let her think the worst. For his mission's sake, at least.

He closed the bag. "How did you get in here?"

"I came through the boiler room. And I know how you got in here," she stated smugly. "Nice wig, by the way."

His mouth quirked. So his instinct that he was being watched had been correct. He should have guessed it was Colleen.

But she was supposed to be at the Vances' this afternoon.

He wondered what she'd say when she was told

he'd been at the Vances' from early afternoon to night-fall and that the whole Vance clan and her own parents would swear he'd been there, not inside the museum.

"You know, *bella,* your snooping's going to cause harm one day. Possibly to yourself. You have no idea what you are walking into." The thought that she could have easily walked in to find Escalante here made him shudder with dread.

"I can take care of myself," she replied, her tone belligerent.

"Do you like danger so much that you're willing to risk your life? Or are you really that naive that you think you can't get hurt because you're only report-ing the news?"

He put the bag down against the wall. "Come, we must go."

"Not without answers, I'm not. What is this? Some kind of hobby? You don't need the money, do you? I thought your family had plenty." She jabbed a finger at him. "You're not into gambling like O'Brien was, are you?"

"No, *bella.*" He took her arm. "We must leave."

She jerked away from him. "Stop calling me that."

He raised an eyebrow. "You don't like to be called beautiful?"

A blush crept up her neck. "Not when you don't mean it."

"But I do mean it," he stated softly.

She spun away and started inspecting the works of art against the wall. "Why are these down here? How did you know they were here?"

She turned narrow eyes on him. "Is that why you've been spending so much time with Dahlia Sainsbury? Is she in on this with you? I could believe she's capable of such deceit, but somehow I'd convinced myself you weren't like that."

Again, his insides bunched at her contemptuous remark. He shouldn't be hurt by her opinion. But deep down he wished he could allow her to think better of him. If only he could tell her the truth. "Colleen, *per favore,* we must go. Now."

"What's this?" she asked as she stepped toward the door.

He'd been wondering the same thing, but had been distracted by the paintings. He hadn't checked the door for security sensors yet. "Colleen, wait!"

Too late—she'd opened the door. With a smirk over her shoulder, she stepped into the yawning darkness.

He put his hands in the air in a frustrated display that was lost on her retreating back. Positive he'd live to regret it, he followed her into the darkness.

In the dirty tunnel an odor Colleen didn't recognize wafted down the shaft from up ahead, where the faintest glow of light brought relief to the blackness.

Behind her, she could hear Alessandro muttering to himself in Italian.

It was probably a good thing she couldn't understand a word of it. No doubt he was berating her. She couldn't keep her mouth from twisting in wry amusement.

"You know, I'm pretty certain this tunnel will connect with the old silver-mining tunnels," she said, keeping her voice low. "This access wasn't here when I was a child."

Contrary to his opinion, she wasn't naive and she knew there were risks involved in investigating. But taking those risks was what made her good at her job and made her job rewarding.

"I didn't realize the tunnels went this far," came Alessandro's hushed reply.

She reached out to touch the dirt walls and felt the fresh, sharp-chiseled marks. "I don't think they originally did. I'm sure these tunnels are fairly new."

Alessandro moved in front of Colleen as they neared the opening of the tunnel. With a hand on her shoulder, he pressed her back toward the wall.

His protective gesture melted some of her disappointment at finding him with a bag full of paintings.

"What do you think this is?" she asked.

Overhead, a string of exposed light bulbs ran across the dirt ceiling. Wooden crates filled the round cavern. A forklift sat off to one side. Another darkened tunnel across the small expanse led to more darkness.

Alessandro shook his head, and put his finger to his mouth. Slowly, she followed him forward to one of the wooden crates. The odor grew stronger.

"What's that smell?" she asked in a hushed voice.

He leaned in next to her ear. "Mothballs."

Ah. She understood. The pungent scent of mothballs would throw off the drug-sniffing dogs at customs.

The markings on the outside noted the crate was shipped to the museum from another museum in France. The crate was nailed shut.

She and Alessandro spread out and checked each crate and found the same thing. Colleen watched Alessandro go to the forklift, rummage around inside the cab and emerge with a long crowbar.

His gaze met hers and though she was still upset at finding him in the process of stealing, she couldn't help the shiver of awareness that taunted her anger. His apprehension didn't bode well and made her nerves edgy.

Alessandro moved to the box in front of her and stuck the clawed end of the bar under the nail.

The noise of moving feet from one of the other tunnels echoed in the small chamber, soft and wispy, yet pronounced by the anxiety charging the air.

Panic welled in Colleen's chest as she grabbed at

Alessandro's arm. His jaw tensed and she could see the frustration in his eyes but he laid the bar down and grabbed her hand and they rushed back into the tunnel from which they'd come.

Her reporter's instincts surging to life, Colleen tried to stop to see who was coming. The information would be crucial.

Alessandro propelled her forward. She clenched her jaw as he practically dragged her away. When they were once again in the basement, he carefully shut the door.

She glared at him. "I wanted to see who was coming."

"Too dangerous. How did you get in?" he asked in a whisper.

He'd never fit through that window, so she shook her head. "We can't go out that way."

He said a harsh word in Italian and then took her hand again. He led her up the stairs. Colleen was surprised to find herself in the curator's office. Alessandro slid a panel shut. Colleen blinked. The wall looked solid. "How did you…?"

"I found the panel when I searched her office," he replied as he picked up his briefcase. He turned to look at Colleen, and then, as if making up his mind, opened his briefcase and pulled out the black wig. "Come here, *bella.* You must wear this."

"Why?"

"Because your blond hair will stand out."

"First, tell me why. I can't just ignore that I found you here, stealing from the museum."

"I promise I will explain, but we must leave now, before those in the tunnels realize that we've been in there and they come looking for us. Trust me when I tell you they'd kill us without any questions."

His tense jaw and sober gaze made her believe him. "But the guard?"

He put the wig on her head. "Saw Dahlia come in and out with me and then enter without me. When he sees us both, I hope he'll think he just wasn't paying enough attention."

"Let's hope," Colleen muttered in agreement, itching at the heavy wig.

"*Sì*, let's." Alessandro grinned. "Come. Walk briskly, but not too fast. We don't want him to get suspicious."

Taking a deep breath, she walked out of the office. With Alessandro at her elbow, they walked to the service door. From somewhere behind them a door opened, then the fall of footsteps on the hardwood floor brought fresh panic, speeding up Colleen's already pounding heart rate.

"Steady now," Alessandro said into her ear, his voice reassuring and thrilling.

"Miss Sainsbury? Miss Sainsbury!" the guard called.

"Keep going," Alessandro urged, as he thrust her through the service door. The wig caught on the latch and flew off her head.

"Hey!" shouted the guard.

A second passed before the museum alarm echoed off the walls. Metal gates descended from the ceiling to click into place in front of the paintings.

Alessandro kept his momentum moving forward. Colleen skidded on the pavement as she tried to stop him from dragging her along. "No. We have to wait for the police. I won't tell them about you, only about the tunnels."

His dark gaze bored into her. He pulled out a gun. "I'm sorry, *bella.*"

Colleen gasped. Disbelief surged through her veins. "Is that standard issue for accountants?"

"Move."

She stood her ground. "No. I promise, I won't say anything about you."

Somewhere in the distance the sound of sirens filled the air.

His shackle-like grip tight, he hauled her toward the corner. "Where's your car?"

"I'm not telling you," she snapped while struggling to break free. "You can't do this!" Outrage throbbed at her temples. How stupid of her to trust her instincts about him.

"Then I'll throw you over my shoulder and carry you," he said roughly.

"You wouldn't dare. Somebody would stop to help me," she declared. She lashed out with her foot and caught him on the shin.

Through gritted teeth, he said, "Not if you're unconscious. I'd just tell anyone who asked that you've had too much to drink."

Not wanting to know how he'd render her unconscious, she decided she had a better chance of escaping his clutches if she stayed conscious. She pointed across the street to the alley. He pulled her along the street toward her car.

"Keys?"

Grudgingly, she withdrew them from her pants pocket. He pushed her in and forced her to scoot over into the passenger seat. He fired up the engine and pulled out of the parking place and jerked to a stop just as a police car screeched to a halt in front of the museum.

"Hang on," he said. Throwing the car into Reverse, he backed down the alley to the next corner, and then the little car shot forward.

Colleen waved her arms in an effort to attract the patrolman's attention, but with the waning light of evening she doubted he could have seen her, even if he'd been looking in her direction.

A horrible sinking feeling settled in the pit of

her stomach as the car hurtled out of sight of the authorities.

"I can't believe you just kidnapped me. You just keep getting lower and lower," she huffed.

When he remained silent, she decided to try to reason with him. Appeal to his sense of family, honor, things she could have sworn he had. Had she truly been wrong about that?

"What about your little girl? Don't you think it will be hard on her to have a daddy in prison?"

He slanted her a sharp glare.

"Wouldn't it be better for her if you did the right thing and turned yourself in? I'm sure your aunt and uncle could get you some help. If you're in trouble with gambling, there are organizations that can help. What about your job with the European Union? You can't want to risk losing everything just to keep me quiet. I've already promised I'll not say anything."

"How about you start keeping that promise to be quiet right now?"

Pressing her lips into a tight line, she glared at him. Alessandro Donato had shown his true colors. Dirty. Rotten. Scoundrel. So much for the superhero image she'd built up in her mind.

Crossing her arms on her chest, she heaved an angry sigh. "You are in *such* hot water."

* * *

Dahlia Sainsbury pulled up to the rustic cabin tucked away in the middle of the woods. Checking her watch, she noted with a grimace she was ten minutes late. Thanks to Alessandro.

Picking her way carefully over the unpaved, pot-holed walkway to the front door, she rapped on the dark wood with her knuckle.

The door swung open and the scents of spicy cumin and fresh cilantro enveloped her. Her mouth watered.

"You're late," snapped the dark-haired man known by those who feared him as *El Jefe.*

To her, he would always be Baltasar Escalante. The man responsible for the death of her beloved half brother, Alistair Barclay. She stepped past Baltasar, dropping her gaze so he wouldn't see the hatred in her eyes. "It couldn't be helped. Too many people have been asking questions. First that annoying Colleen Montgomery came to see me."

The door shut with a loud bang. "Well, if you'd done your job in the first place, you wouldn't have to deal with her."

Dahlia's lips tightened. It wasn't her fault Donato was a clumsy oaf, albeit a handsome one, and had spilled the poison meant for Colleen. "But I did learn something of interest when she came to see me today."

Waving her into the kitchen, he said, "Tell me."

On the counter next to the cooking food lay a small square flat mirror with four lines of white powder. Obviously Baltasar had been sampling their product again.

A heightened sense of anxiety plucked at her nerves.

She watched him pick up a knife and begin chopping vegetables. Him and a knife. Not a comfortable feeling.

"She's got a thing for Donato."

He grunted. "How does that help my plans?"

"It could prove useful," she said with a shrug.

He didn't respond. Instead he seemed fixated on the task of cooking. Chopping, scooping, frying. But that was how he was. Especially when high. Obsessive, compulsive, evil.

He laid the knife down and moved to the sink. She stared at the gleaming blade, dripping with tomato juice. She could imagine herself grasping the black handle and driving the metal tip into his wiry back. She could picture deep-red blood oozing from the wound as he lay withering in agony, feel the promise of joy that would flood through her.

Her breathing turned shallow, her hand flexed. No. It wasn't time yet. She had to wait. She wanted him to suffer, but she wanted it to be a long and drawn-out affair. She wanted to see his face when he realized she had the power to destroy him.

Soon. Very soon.

She looked up and met his dark, intense gaze. Repressing a shudder of distaste for him, she smiled. A coy, inviting smile that never failed to draw him in.

He stalked forward, like the predator he was, and took her into his arms. He buried his face against her neck, nipping at the tender flesh there. She closed her eyes, glad he couldn't see the revulsion that his touch brought.

"I fear Alessandro Donato knows something, but what, I'm not sure. He's been sniffing around," she murmured.

"So, let him sniff. He'll find nothing," came Baltasar's muffled reply. He slipped her jacket from her shoulders, his fingertips lingering on her shoulders.

"Your dinner will burn," she said, hoping for a reprieve.

He leaned back, his hand reaching up to release her hair from its bonds. "It needs to simmer. Just as I've been simmering while we've been apart."

"He has a child."

Baltasar abruptly pulled away. His black eyes narrowed in interest. "A child?"

The reprieve she wanted. Her lips curved. "Yes."

"A child." He began to pace. "What about *my* child?" His gravelly voice rose, the rage making each syllable vibrate like a rattler about to strike.

"Those Vances have my child and I will not rest until I have him back."

"It's best if you lay low for a while longer," she stated quietly, cautiously.

His expression twisted. The lover replaced with the maniacal madman, who arranged for bombings and killings without any remorse. A man both feared and hated.

"Lay low? Like some scoundrel dog? Never! The Vances and Montgomerys will pay for their deeds." His rage escalated, his voice rising a painful octave. "Oh, yes. They'll pay."

He pounded his fist into his hand, punctuating each phrase. "The drugs are on the street, weakening society. After we move this next shipment, I'll find a way to get my son back."

In a swift movement, he picked up the knife and slammed the sharp tip into the cutting board. "Soon, those who have tried to destroy me will see the full extent of my power."

She waited a beat for a diabolical laugh that chilled her bones. She wasn't ready for him to do something that would get him caught. She had plans of her own that needed to be seen to fruition. That the Vance and Montgomery families suffered in the process of her own agenda was an added benefit, for they also held some of the blame for Alistair's death.

If the two meddling families hadn't interfered, Alistair wouldn't have gone to prison.

But it was on Escalante's order that Alistair be killed. He would be made to suffer.

"Maybe you should accompany me to London. I have a dealer there who has found a Degas. You love Degas," she said, her voice now soft and cajoling.

He stilled. "Degas?"

The distraction worked.

"Hmm. Yes, I love Degas." He snorted a line of cocaine and then walked to the stove. "No more talk of this tonight. We eat. Tomorrow the wheels of revenge will turn again."

"Indeed, they will."

NINE

You are in such *hot water.*

Colleen's parting words reverberated in Alessandro's head.

Like a lobster in a pot, he silently retorted.

Bringing Colleen into the mix was a breach of security. Kidnapping her would likely send him to jail. But what choice had he?

If he let her go to the authorities, he'd lose his chance to capture and take down the man ultimately responsible for his wife's death. He'd spent too many years and too much time tracking the evil drug lord to be this close and miss the opportunity to finally stop Escalante.

Leading Colleen by the hand through the kitchen of the Broadmoor Hotel and into the service elevator, Alessandro acknowledged the only course of action now was to tell Colleen everything. He could only hope she'd realize the importance of his mission and not splash the story across the front page of the newspaper.

Not that he could expect her to keep quiet forever, but at least until Escalante was captured. Then she could tell whatever tales she chose.

"How did that just happen?" Colleen groused as the elevator ascended toward the penthouse floor.

"Scusi?"

"Not one person even batted an eye as we came in. You'd think someone would have stopped us to ask what we were doing in the staff-only section of the hotel. Who are you?"

"I'll explain in a moment."

Colleen planted her hands on her hips. "I want an explanation *now.*"

She was a beauty when fired up. "Patience, *bella.* The walls have ears."

She frowned pointedly as her gaze took in the seemingly bare, empty elevator. But she didn't say another word until they were in his suite.

The main room boasted elegance with plush beige carpet and rich mahogany furniture tastefully accented in warm blues and greens. A full wall of windows overlooking the city gave the living room an expansive feel. Two sets of French doors opened to large bedrooms, each with a luxuriant king-size bed.

She whistled. "Nice. Apparently international accountants do better than the local variety."

The web of secrets between them would soon be dismantled, he thought thankfully. He didn't like the flush of guilt washing over him. He shrugged off his jacket and laid it on the back of a wing-back chair. "*Cara mia,* take a seat."

Her blue eyes regarded him with distrust. "I don't think I will. You'd better tell me what's going on."

"*Sì,* brother. Do tell us what's going on," Tomas said from the archway leading into the dining room where he leaned against the doorjamb.

He had on the khaki pants and dress shirt he'd left the suite in earlier. His relaxed stance was nothing more than an illusion. Alessandro saw the tightness of his brother's jaw and the hard glint in his brown eyes.

Alessandro's stomach plummeted as Colleen's eyes rounded in shock. Her gaze jumped from his brother to him and back again. She looked as though she might faint, and somewhere in the back of Alessandro's mind lurked the thought that her passing out could work to his advantage. If she did, he could deny the existence of his brother in order to keep Tomas's cover from being blown.

But Alessandro had a sinking feeling he wasn't going to be able to keep her in the dark any longer. She'd dig up the truth on her own and get hurt. His heart twisted at the thought.

"*Cara mia,* my brother, Tomas. Tomas, Colleen." Tomas glided forward, his loafers making no noise on the lush carpet. He took Colleen's hand and kissed her knuckles. Alessandro's stomach muscles clenched and he resisted the urge to place a possessive arm around Colleen.

"My pleasure, *signorina*," Tomas purred, his accent heavier than normal, an affectation Alessandro and Tomas both used when wanting to keep a woman off balance. For some odd reason women found their native tongue appealing. Alessandro wanted to box his brother's ears for laying on the charm. They didn't normally compete for the attention of a woman. He didn't want to start now.

Colleen shook her head and disengaged her hand. "Brothers. This makes so much sense."

She turned her sharp, intelligent gaze on Alessandro. "No wonder it seemed that you were in two places at once."

She studied him for a moment then stared at Tomas. "Up close and together, I can see the subtle differences. Fraternal twins?"

Tomas grinned. "No. Alessandro's my big brother."

"Couldn't be by much," Colleen said.

"Sometimes I wonder," Alessandro replied, sending Tomas a disapproving glare for revealing himself.

"Interesting." She crossed her arms over her chest. "I'm waiting for that explanation."

Tomas sat on the couch and stretched out his legs. "This should be good."

Alessandro shot him a glare. "I had no choice but to bring her here. We found Escalante's drug warehouse."

"That's great!" Tomas exclaimed.

"Escalante?" Colleen frowned, clearly puzzled. "But he's dead."

Alessandro shook his head. "They never recovered his body from the plane crash. We've tracked him through Europe and back to here. We believe he had plastic surgery, and that is why he can move about without anyone knowing who he is."

Colleen's eyes widened. "So he's *El Jefe?*"

"Sì."

"Where is the warehouse?" asked Tomas.

"Who's *we?*" Colleen asked and gestured with her finger at the two brothers.

"Under the museum and *we* being Interpol," Alessandro said, answering them both.

"Ah, so your hunch about Dahlia Sainsbury was correct," Tomas said, admiration lacing his words.

"Sì." Having his instincts about Dahlia validated felt good.

"I knew it," Colleen muttered.

Alessandro ignored her comment and tried to focus once again on the problem at hand. "I swiped her security card to get into the museum. It's only a matter of time before she realizes it's gone and alerts Escalante. I need to get back to that warehouse and capture him."

"We'll need backup. I'll call Falcon." Tomas rose and strode into the bedroom.

Reeling from this conversation, Colleen sat down on the vacated couch. "Let me get this straight. You and your *brother* work for *Interpol* and are tracking down *Escalante*, who you believe is still at large and operating in Colorado Springs."

"*Sì, bella.*"

Her mind went back to the night Holly had confided in her about Alessandro's heroics. He'd saved Colleen's brother and sister-in-law from certain death. He was one of the good guys. A superhero.

Now he was after Escalante. A madman, a murderer. Her heart pounded at the implications. The possibilities. The risks. "This is even more huge than I thought."

Alessandro crouched down in front of her and took her hands. His warm palms sent ripples of sensation up her arms. "*Cara mia,* you must understand how sensitive this information is. If Escalante realizes we are on to him, there's no telling what he'll do. We must find him before he discovers Manuel Vance is his son."

She'd forgotten about little Manuel's parentage. The child had become such a part of Peter and

Emily's life that it didn't seem there was a time when Manuel hadn't been their child. Colleen swallowed. "I wouldn't do anything to put Manuel in danger."

"Good." His eyes held hers for a only a second, as if he didn't need to search for her trustworthiness, as if there was no doubt. Then his gaze drifted across her face to her mouth.

Colleen struggled to stay focused when all she wanted to do was lean forward and press her lips to his. She swallowed. "So...so how does Dahlia Sainsbury figure in all this?"

One side of his generous mouth lifted in a crooked smile before he moved to sit beside her. "Thanks to Interpol's extensive network, we know Dahlia is Alistair Barclay's half sister, and, we believe, Escalante's accomplice. Alistair used his hotels as a cover for the drug activity. Dahlia may be using the museum for the same purposes."

Colleen stared. "But Sam said the authorities were convinced Escalante ordered the hit on Barclay."

"*Sì. La Mano Oscura,* the drug cartel, has long arms, even ones that can penetrate prison walls."

"And she's his...ugh, that's gross. Obviously, she didn't have much regard for Alistair." If anyone were to hurt someone she loved, Colleen knew she'd stop at nothing to bring that person down.

"Perhaps she does not know. Or she could be as

evil as he is. Escalante's charisma is very strong. He's a powerful man in many ways. He uses manipulation and blackmail freely, without remorse. I do not know yet what motivates Dahlia, but I do know she finds you a threat and will pay in the end for trying to hurt you."

Surprised at the heat in his gaze and the raw determination in his voice, her pulse skipped a jagged jig. "What are you talking about?"

"The night of the museum gala, Dahlia tainted your punch with what I believe was poison."

Colleen's heart thumped in her chest. "So that's why you knocked the glass from my hand."

He caressed her cheek. "*Sì*, I could not let her hurt you."

Deep warmth invaded her like sun breaking through an oppressive cloud. "You saved my life."

He smiled slightly. "Your investigations must have been getting too close to the truth. Escalante had Neil O'Brien murdered and tried to frame you. If Dahlia had succeeded in killing you, then she and Escalante would have mistakenly believed they would have been safe from further scrutiny."

He could rationalize all he wanted. The fact remained that he'd acted unselfishly and bravely when he hadn't needed to. "I thank you for saving my life as well as Jake's and Holly's."

He arched a dark brow. "You know?"

She touched his arm, needing to reach out to him, to convey the growing feelings inside that she declined to put names to. "Yes. Holly told me the night of the gala. She refused to believe the rumors that you had anything to do with Mayor Vance's shooting. But she told only me and I promised her I wouldn't say anything until I could confirm for myself that you weren't involved. I know now that you weren't."

"*Bella,* you must not tell anyone of my life."

A rock landed in the hollow of her stomach. "This is a story that people will want to know. That people deserve to know. You're a hero."

A pained, dark expression crossed his face. "I'm no one's hero." He stood. "I understand your need for a story, but not before *La Mano Oscura* is completely wiped out."

"Agreed. I wouldn't do anything to compromise your investigation. But after…" She shook her head, making no promises.

He gave a resigned sigh.

"Why are you so passionate about this?"

His jaw tensed. "It's personal."

"Does this have to do with your wife and daughter?"

A shuttered look entered his eyes. "I—"

"Bad news," Tomas said as he entered the living room and cut off what Alessandro had started to say.

Frustration arched through Colleen. She so

wanted to know more about this man who could very well be a modern-day knight in shining armor.

Alessandro ran a hand through his hair. "What now?"

Tomas grimaced. "Falcon agrees we need to seize the warehouse. He wants you to stay here with Colleen and keep her out of sight until we find Escalante."

"Perché?" Alessandro's frown changed his countenance to dark and dangerous.

Colleen drew back slightly. Could she really trust this man with her heart or her life? His obsession with Escalante and the drug cartel went beyond his work with Interpol. Personal, he'd said. In what way?

Tomas's dark eyes regarded Colleen steadily. "An arrest warrant has been issued for you."

Colleen jerked to her feet. "Why?"

"Falcon is looking into the matter. But for now you must stay here or you both will be arrested."

Flustered, Colleen looked at Alessandro. "The guard at the museum."

Alessandro nodded. "Perhaps. Falcon will let us know."

"Who is this Falcon person? How do you know you can trust him?" Colleen asked.

Tomas and Alessandro exchanged glances. Alessandro spoke. "Falcon is our CIA contact here in the States. Extremely trustworthy."

Colleen rubbed at her temples. "So now what?"

"We will, as you say, hang out for a while. It has been a vigorous day. You should rest," Alessandro said, concern evident in his dark gaze.

A pleasant warmth grew inside her. How did he do that? Fill her with doubts one minute and then send her pulse rocketing toward the sky the next.

"I'm too keyed up for resting. But I am hungry. Can we at least order room service?" she asked.

Much to her amusement, both brothers became very solicitous. Tomas offered to order their meal, while Alessandro prepared Colleen a cold club soda with a slice of lime. They then ushered her out to the balcony.

The sun was just beginning to set on the horizon. The golden glow bounced off the Rocky Mountains, painting the sky with vivid swirling hues of pink, orange and purple. A light breeze brought freshness to the air and seemed to lift the tension from her body as she sank down onto a comfortable chair.

Alessandro placed their glasses on the small square glass-topped table between them before folding himself into an identical chair. His presence sent little sparks of excitement running up her spine. They were alone in a romantic setting. She should have been nervous or at least a little anxious, but she felt alive. And it was a good feeling.

In the background, Colleen heard Tomas on the

phone ordering a scrumptious-sounding meal. Her stomach growled at the thought of food. She smiled sheepishly to Alessandro.

"Food will arrive soon. The kitchen is fast," he commented as he took a sip of his soda.

Colleen took a drink from her glass. The refreshing bite of the bubbly soda went down smoothly. "This is nice out here."

"Hmm," he murmured.

They sat in companionable silence for a moment. With a sigh of contentment, Colleen closed her eyes and rested her head against the cushion of the chair. She shouldn't feel so relaxed and comfortable. So safe.

Life was spinning out of control around her. People were trying to kill her, the police wanted to arrest her and Alessandro had kidnapped her. Yet here she was, totally at ease with the handsome man beside her, a glass of refreshing soda and a meal on the way.

She could get used to this.

Relaxation was a luxury she rarely allowed herself. Staying on top of the news required total commitment of time and energy.

Opening her eyes, she found Alessandro watching her.

The tender expression in his gaze froze the smile tugging at the corners of her mouth and made her heart pound.

I could not let her hurt you.

His earlier words played themselves over in her mind. Not being one to dance around any subject, she asked, "What did you mean when you said you couldn't let Dahlia hurt me?"

One side of his sensuous mouth curved upward into a crooked smile. "I've grown rather fond of you."

She blinked. "Fond?"

He reached out and encased her hand in his big, strong grip. Slowly, he turned her palm up and placed a gentle kiss in the center, setting off a delightful shiver that tightened her scalp and heated her cheeks. "*Cara mia,* you are a beautiful, courageous and admirable woman."

His words spread pleasure through her, blanketing all the lonely and insecure places like melted butter on toast. Her gaze dropped to his mouth and she found herself tilting forward, drawn by an invisible thread toward something that seemed at once forbidden and yet seemed so natural.

Their lips met tentatively and somewhere in her mind she wondered if he were as nervous about the meaning of this kiss as she was.

A knock on the outer door pulled them apart.

In the waning evening light, Alessandro's dark eyes reflected stunned confusion mingled with yearning. Her lips tingled and restlessness washed through her, making her wish the kiss had lasted longer.

He rose and extended his hand to help her to her feet. His big palm firmly and securely embraced her smaller hand. They stood toe to toe, gazing into each other's eyes, and a flutter of sensation expanded in her chest. "I'm fond of you, too," she admitted softly.

The expression in his dark eyes weakened her knees. Affection blossomed in her chest. She tried to temper the feeling. This man challenged her, thrilled her and made her feel special enough to let him in. But letting him in would open her up to the vulnerability of loss. To the scary proposition of risking her heart. She wasn't sure she was capable of ever doing that. Not even for Alessandro.

Alessandro forced his feet to move forward toward the dining area where Tomas and the waiter were setting up their meal. All he wanted to do was pull Colleen to him and continue the kiss they'd shared.

He'd told her he was fond of her. But *fond* was too mild a word for the feelings rocketing through his system. These feelings and emotions were more than he could handle with Colleen beside him talking to his brother.

Alessandro needed space and time to sort out this mess he'd allowed to happen. Colleen shouldn't be here. He should have kept a distance from her, should have realized he was too emotionally involved with her to keep her at arm's length.

But he didn't want her at arm's length. He wanted her beside him; he wanted to protect her, cherish her. Love her.

His mind rebelled against that thought. He'd sworn that after Paola he'd never lay his heart bare for any woman to crush again. Paola's use of drugs was a choice she'd made, a choice that had cut him to the quick, permanently scarring his soul. And though he ultimately held Escalante and his drug cartel responsible, Alessandro's heart had been brutally betrayed by Paola, his wife.

Alessandro had to remember his purpose; he had to continue on his mission to seek justice, for Mia's sake. He would never be able to be the father he should be until he could look his daughter in the eye and know that he'd avenged her mother's death.

Colleen could only distract him from that goal.

But now he felt a guilt weighing on him for letting the relationship with Colleen move in a direction he had no intention of going.

After they ate and could once again find a moment alone, he would explain to Colleen why a relationship between them could never work.

No matter how much he wished otherwise.

TEN

"What about the time you slipped a toad into Mama's bed?" Tomas's eyes twinkled with humor as he regarded his brother. To Colleen he said, "You should have seen the way Mama flew out of the house screaming."

"Ha! What about when Papa found you stuck in a tree with a skunk standing guard? Now, that was funny. Even after the skunk left you refused to come down. Papa had to climb up and get you and nearly fell out of the tree when he smelled you."

Tomas shrugged. "I was six. I thought it was a cat at first."

Colleen laughed until tears seeped from her eyes. She so enjoyed the friendly bantering between the two Donato brothers. For the whole course of their meal, they'd regaled her with stories of their childhood in Italy.

She in turn had shared a few of her childhood's

most colorful adventures and relished the laughter and camaraderie of the time spent with Alessandro and Tomas.

A loud beeping came from the bedroom off to the right. Tomas pushed back his chair. "The fax."

He strode from the room, leaving Colleen and Alessandro alone.

"You and your brother have a good relationship," she commented.

Alessandro nodded. "*Sì*. I can always count on Tomas to cover my back."

"That's how my brothers and I are. We could fight like the dickens, but we always watched out for each other."

Colleen smiled as they shared the moment. Her gaze dropped to his lips and her breathing quickened as she remembered the feel of his lips on hers. She had half a mind to move around the table and plant herself in his lap and beg for another kiss just to prove that his kiss really wasn't all that spectacular.

Or maybe to prove that his kiss *was* that spectacular?

She met his gaze. The deep connection that passed between them left her with the distinct impression that somehow he knew what she'd been thinking. Instinctively, she leaned toward him, wishing the barrier of the table would disappear and she could once again feel his arms around her.

Abruptly, he stood, his expression shifting, closing her out. She drew her eyebrows together in confusion.

He rounded the table and held out his hand to her. "Come, let us retire to the balcony to watch the stars fill the sky."

Fitting her hand into his, she allowed him to lead her out to the balcony. Instead of sitting, she moved to the railing and leaned against the cool metal.

The rising moon shone brightly in the cloudless, darkening sky. A million diamonds twinkled in the heavens. A soft breeze ruffled her ponytail. She closed her eyes briefly and said a silent prayer of thanksgiving to God for everything. Her family, her safety, Alessandro.

Awareness slipped over her like a cool satin sheet as Alessandro came to stand beside her. His shoulder bumped against hers and she leaned slightly into him.

"Cold?" He slipped an arm around her shoulders.

Taking pleasure in the warmth of his tall stature and his protective embrace, she relaxed against him. "Hmm, not now."

"There's something…something I must say," Alessandro stated softly, his breath tickling the hair at her temple.

She turned her face toward him. His lips were so close. "Yes?"

He cleared his throat. "I must apologize for earlier."

She frowned. She couldn't think of a thing he owed her an apology for. "For what?"

"For kissing you. I do not want to lead you on. There can never be a future for us," he said, his voice low and full of regret.

Stunned by his words and by the hurt and disappointment flooding through her, she stepped back. His arm fell away from her shoulders, taking his warmth and robbing her of every iota of peace she'd been feeling.

She blinked rapidly against the unnatural stinging in her eyes and went on the offensive. "You think an awful lot of yourself, Mr. Donato. Who said I wanted a future with you? Just because we shared one little kiss doesn't mean I had fantasies of marrying you. Talk about an ego trip."

He gave her a wry smile. "My mistake, *bella*." He bowed slightly. "My apologies."

"You got that straight." Colleen paced away, willing the turmoil going on inside her chest to quiet down. She stopped and turned to face him. "Just for argument's sake, why wouldn't a future work for us? Because of your daughter?"

He stared up at the moon. "There are many reasons. Mia is one of them."

Putting aside her own feelings and shifting into

investigator mode, she stepped closer and softened her voice to a coaxing tenor. "Tell me about Mia."

The faint light of the moon revealed his tender expression. "She's a sweet child. Bubbly, full of laughter. She has her mother's smile."

Colleen's heart twisted with a jolt of jealousy, which she quickly subdued. "Her mother was your late wife?"

Turning away, he stalked to the chair and slowly sat down. With his elbows on his knees, he dropped his head into his hands.

Concern sliced through Colleen. She went to him. "Alessandro?"

He lifted his gaze and she sucked in a breath at the torture in his dark eyes reflected in the moon's glow. "Paola and I were very young when we married. She was a wild girl. Beautiful, full of life, yet a darkness lurked in her soul. I thought I could tame her, that I could bring her into the light of my love. God's love. I knew her casual use of drugs would lead to addiction and I tried everything I could to keep her away from them. But she loved the high more than she loved me."

Sympathy slammed into Colleen's chest, forcing her to sit in the vacant chair beside Alessandro or fall to the ground. Wincing against the pain emanating from his soul, she laid a hand on his shoulder, offering what comfort she could. "I'm so sorry."

"She left without telling me she was carrying my child. I didn't find out about Mia until after Paola's overdose."

"Oh, no." Outrage and sympathy on his behalf clogged her throat as tears filled her eyes. She couldn't imagine how devastating that must have been, to find out his wife had OD'd and then to discover he had a daughter. "Where is Mia now?"

"With friends."

"Why not with your family?"

"Safer if no one knows about her."

"Wait a second." Colleen shook her head in confusion. "Safer for whom?"

"Mia, my family. Me. I have a job to do and I won't rest until it's done."

"A job? What could be more important than raising your daughter? How can you deny her existence? How can you deny your family the opportunity to have your child in their lives?" She stood up. "Your responsibility is to your child. Not to some job."

"You don't understand. I can't be a father to Mia until justice is served." He rose, a towering figure full of suppressed rage. "I swore I'd take down the man who supplied the drugs to Paola. The man behind *La Mano Oscura*."

"Escalante," she stated softly. His passionate pursuit of the drug lord now made sense. But his reasons were woefully misguided.

"Yes, Escalante." He spat out the name. "His operation in Amsterdam provided the drugs that Paola overdosed on. I will not rest until I have justice for her death."

"But it's not your place to take vengeance."

"If I don't, who will? Who will see that justice is done for all the innocent victims who have succumbed to the drugs Escalante pushes?"

She could hardly believe he was saying these things. She raised her eyebrows. "First of all, these *victims,* as you call them, are far from innocent. Each person is given a choice. Your wife chose to abuse her body with drugs. No one forced her. That she would choose such a life over your love is unfathomable to me, but it was her choice. Second, only God can give out true justice."

"I hardly need a lecture from you on God. I can never be as strong in my faith as you. I grew up believing that God was true and just. But I've seen too much pain, too much darkness, to find the faith to think that God will deal with men like Escalante. God is beyond me and has been for a long time."

Saddened by his words, Colleen searched for a way to make him understand God's unfailing love. She realized with sickening clarity that she'd taken her faith for granted. That she hadn't spent enough time delving into God's word to effectively champion Him to Alessandro when it counted the most.

Oh, Father in Heaven, give me the words to reach him.

"Alessandro, God isn't beyond you. He loves you. He loves Mia. He wants what's best for you both."

She reached out to touch his arm, his muscles rigid under her palm. "But Alessandro, He won't move in your life until you seek Him. He gives us a choice. You have to choose Him, not revenge."

Alessandro ran a finger gently down her cheek and pressed lightly on her lips. "You have such a good heart."

Her breath hitched. She wanted to move into his embrace, to hug him to her and hold on tight until all the demons from his past were wiped away. She ached to heal his battered soul and his wounded heart. To show him that if given the chance, *she* would choose him.

But he dropped his hand and went back inside, leaving her alone with the shock of knowing that she would choose him over the fear of loss.

No one could predict the future. God's word stated that each day had enough worries of its own, therefore we shouldn't worry about tomorrow. Worry and fear wouldn't add time to our lives. Each day was a gift to be lived to its fullest potential.

Colleen stayed on the terrace in prayerful contemplation for several minutes. Finally, deciding she needed to connect with Alessandro, not for the sake of her story, but for the sake of her heart, she went inside.

In the dining room, the dinner dishes had been cleared away and replaced with two large, dark duffel bags unzipped to expose the contents. Her stomach lurched. Inside were weapons and ropes and the other paraphernalia that went along with a tactical situation.

Tomas and Alessandro had changed into all-black clothing, looking like twin versions of some character from a James Bond flick. She froze, assessing the situation. "You're going back there now?"

"*Sì.*" Alessandro barely spared her a glance as he zipped the bags shut. "We must. Dahlia was spotted at her apartment, so we can assume that she hasn't discovered her missing security access card. But she will."

"I'm coming with you," Colleen stated.

Alessandro exchanged a meaningful glance with Tomas before coming to her and taking her hands. "*Cara mia,* you must understand. This is too dangerous. You will only get in the way and be a distraction that could result in injury."

Bristling, Colleen yanked her hands from his. "Understand? Get in the way? You think that little of me?"

Alessandro sighed. "No, *bella.* You twist my words."

"I don't think so. You see me as some helpless

female who needs big bad you to keep her safe. Well, let me tell you something. I'm capable of taking care of myself. I've gone into situations that would make most men wimp out. I've faced danger and not blinked an eye. I won't get in your way. I'll let you be the hero—I just want the scoop."

She'd like to think she wanted to go with him for her story, her career. This would be a plum opportunity. But deep down she wanted to go because she wanted to stay close to him, to make sure he stayed safe.

He closed his eyes briefly as if pained. When he opened his eyes, a lethal calmness in his dark gaze sent a shiver over her skin. She saw not the warm and caring man whom she'd come to know, but the Interpol agent ready to do battle. "No. I will not allow it."

"I don't like to be told what to do," she huffed.

He lifted his shoulder in a careless shrug. "Too bad."

Colleen's jaw dropped. How dare he dismiss her so easily? She glanced at Tomas. He gave her an apologetic look but there was no compromise in his eyes.

Fisting her hands, she watched as each man slung a bag over a shoulder and headed for the door. Colleen grabbed her purse, intending to follow them out. They might not want her with them, but they couldn't keep her from following them.

At the door, Alessandro motioned for Tomas to

precede him and then Alessandro dropped his bag and put his hands on her shoulders, stopping her in her tracks.

"You must stay here," he said.

"No," she said with a great big dose of defiance.

He stared into her eyes and she lifted her chin in challenge. His expression softened slightly and a smile tugged at the corners of his mouth. "So much spirit and passion. You are a wonder, Colleen Montgomery."

Blinking at his unexpected words, Colleen opened her mouth to say something. But the words left her head as he pulled her to him and she melted beneath the onslaught of his mouth covering hers. She wrapped her arms around his waist and hung on for dear life.

She didn't like the nagging feeling that this could be the last time he ever held her. Suddenly the thought of never seeing him again struck panic in her soul.

The fear of loving and losing strangled her, causing tears to burn the back of her eyes. She tried to hold on to God's word. But how could she control the worry, the fear gripping her?

Slowly, he extracted himself from her. She swayed on her feet, her head dizzy from his kiss and the fear clogging her throat.

He picked up his bag, stepped into the hall and gently shut the door in her face.

"Hey!" She yanked on the handle but it wouldn't budge. Realization exploded in shades of red and yellow. He'd locked her in! Anger brought welcome relief from the torment of fear. She banged on the door with her fist. "Let me out!"

To dope her with a mind-bending kiss and then leave her in a gilded cage like some fragile bird was beyond mean.

"Of all the nerve," she muttered to herself as she stalked to the phone in the living room.

She picked up the receiver, intending to call one of her brothers. There was no dial tone. The phone was plugged into the wall jack but he'd somehow cut the service. The wretch.

He thought he was so smart. She'd show him. She dug around inside her bag and came up empty. He'd taken her cell phone with him. Frustration beat a steady rhythm behind her eyes.

"The sneak!" she yelled and grabbed the square accent pillow from the couch and threw it across the room, then flung herself down to slump on the couch. Great. She'd lost the chance to get the scoop on the story of Escalante's takedown.

Now what? She had to sit here and wait, praying that Alessandro and Tomas didn't get themselves killed.

A shudder of horror assaulted her as the gravity of the situation made itself clear. They were walking into the lion's den without backup. Alessandro wouldn't pray for his own well-being. It was up to her to plead for his safety. She slipped from the couch to her knees and began to pray.

And though losing the opportunity to further her career with a scoop was a blow, losing Alessandro would do her in.

ELEVEN

Entering the museum undetected a second time proved trickier than the first. Outside, guards stood watch at the entrances and Alessandro assumed the guard inside, along with others, would be more alert now.

Luckily, the wiring to the museum was located on the dark side of the building. They were able to approach undetected. Tomas attached a small computerized device to the wires that ran feed to the security cameras.

He recorded five minute's worth of the quiet museum then switched the security cameras to a looping feed of the recorded time.

Using the access card lifted from Dahlia, Alessandro and Tomas entered the building and quickly made their way to Dahlia's office, where Alessandro picked the lock. They slipped inside and, opening the panel in the wall, descended the stairs to the basement.

Once there, Alessandro silently showed Tomas the paintings he'd discovered earlier. Finally they entered the tunnel. A faint light led the way through the carved-out hole. As they neared the opening, they saw men of varying ages and ethnic backgrounds packing up the crates and loading them onto small handcarts.

The handcarts were then being wheeled out of the widened cavern through the tunnel opposite to where Alessandro and Tomas hid in the shadows.

Realizing the men would soon be gone and the opportunity to get Escalante could be lost, Alessandro and Tomas knew they had to move. Alessandro grabbed the cell phone at his waist. No bars appeared on the side of the phone's small screen. They had no way of signaling for backup.

Logic said they should retreat, but the need for justice stayed Alessandro's feet.

He thought about Colleen, safely locked in his suite at the Broadmoor. Having her near would distract him and one of them would end up hurt. Or worse, dead. This way, whatever did happen, he was assured she'd be safe.

After the last man had disappeared, the two brothers dashed across the cavern and entered the dark tunnel made of earth and wooden beams. They stayed discreetly back so as not to alert the men ahead of them.

Pressing themselves to the mud wall, they saw the tunnel end at another cavern where a man stood in the center, barking out orders.

Though the man was definitely not the suave Latino who'd once ruled *La Mano Oscura,* he was of Hispanic descent, with a wide nose and prominent cheek bones. His raspy voice spoke of damage to the vocal chords. From cancer or possibly a fiery plane crash? Alessandro's gut screamed that this man was Escalante.

Alessandro alerted Tomas to his suspicion with a gesture. Tomas gave a sharp affirmative nod. Tension coiled in Alessandro's veins as he waited for the prime moment to strike, when the odds were in their favor.

This was the part of his job that he found invigorating and addictive. Adrenaline revved through him.

Time ticked by. Alessandro saw his moment as the last two of Escalante's henchmen took a cart down yet another dark tunnel. Alessandro motioned to Tomas with practiced hand signals.

Ducking behind the last few remaining carts, Alessandro moved forward. Positioning himself with a clear view of the tunnels, he rose, weapon drawn, and zeroed in on his mark. He was *finally* getting the man responsible for his wife's death. Justice *would* prevail. "Raise your hands so I can see them!"

Escalante turned, his dark eyes assessing Alessandro first with surprise then a sinister glee. Hatred twisted in Alessandro's gut, clouding his judgment. He cocked the hammer back.

"Well, well. What have we here?" Escalante's gravelly voice seeped into the dirt walls.

"I said, raise your hands!" Alessandro repeated, only too glad to have the man disobey the order and give a reason to shoot.

Escalante slowly complied. "See, I'm no threat to you."

Alessandro moved in closer, aware of Tomas opening a crate. Alessandro's heart pounded as victory loomed close at hand. He pulled out a set of handcuffs. He'd take great pleasure in securing his quarry.

A shouted warning from Tomas sent Alessandro into a crouched defensive stance as men rushed into the cavern. Escalante darted behind a crate. Shots rang out from different directions. Some from Tomas, most from the men rushing in.

Alessandro went after Escalante but found himself outnumbered and outgunned. He froze. Defeat burned a hole through his soul, searing his senses with torturous rage.

Escalante took a gun from the hands of one of his henchmen and aimed at Alessandro's heart. "Now we'll see who's in control here." He turned and headed down the tunnel. Over his shoulder he called, "Bring them."

Alessandro's gut clenched. They had Tomas.

Guilt and fury coiled around Alessandro's lungs. Not only had he failed his wife but now his brother, as well.

Rough hands grabbed, twisted and dragged Alessandro forward through the dark, dank tunnel. He fought for release, landing a few satisfying hits on his captors.

They emerged in yet another cavern, lit with bare bulbs strung along the ceiling. A table and chairs showed that this was obviously the meeting room for Escalante's operation.

Two men dragged Tomas into view. His head lolled at an angle; blood and dirt marred his features. A dark stain spread across his chest and blood dripped from his fingertips.

"Tomas! Tomas!" Alessandro called, hoping, praying his brother was still alive and knowing that even if he were, if he didn't receive help soon he would more than likely die. *Oh, Lord, please don't let Tomas die!*

Alessandro thrashed against the hands holding him. Several punches slammed into his gut and jaw. Lights exploded behind his eyes. His knees buckled. He was pushed into a chair, his hands yanked painfully behind his back. Duct tape was stretched tautly around his wrists and ankles, binding him. He fought against the restraints.

"What do we do with him, *El Jefe?*" asked one of the men holding Tomas upright.

Escalante shrugged, then pinned his wild gaze on Alessandro. "Your friend is badly hurt, no?" He walked over to Tomas and placed the barrel of the gun in his hand against Tomas's head. "Should we put him out of his misery?"

Alessandro's heart pounded wildly in his chest and his breath seized in his lungs. Nothing he said would stop Escalante if he wanted to pull the trigger. Alessandro remained silent.

Escalante studied him for a long moment. "Who do you work for?"

Alessandro shook his head. Escalante cocked the gun. Alessandro shivered with rage. "Interpol."

Escalante eased the hammer back into place. "Interesting. Possibly useful."

Alessandro sought for ways to distract Escalante from Tomas. "How did you survive the plane crash, Escalante?"

The man froze. A fierce light gleamed from his insidious eyes. "What did you call me?"

A small sense of victory bolstered Alessandro's spirit. "Baltasar Escalante. That's who you are. I can smell your stench like a gutter rat."

Bellowing in rage like an animal, Escalante

rushed at Alessandro. He swung the gun in a wide arc. The butt of the gun smashed into Alessandro's face. Pain erupted in his right cheek and eye.

Escalante's chest heaved with his exertion. Alessandro stayed focused on the madman, realizing the possibility that he and Tomas would get out of the old mining tunnels alive was nonexistent. He hadn't been able to do God's work. He wouldn't be bringing Escalante to justice.

Despair tore through him. He'd never again see Mia's sweet smile or Colleen's blue eyes. All because of Escalante.

Hatred overshadowed the despair and obscured his senses. "You didn't answer me. How did you survive?"

Escalante took a deep breath, obviously gathering his control. His mouth formed a sinister grin. "I'm like a cat. Nine lives."

"Why did you come back to Colorado Springs? You could have gone anywhere and no one would have known."

Steely determination chiseled his face into hard lines. "I want my son."

Alessandro had been right to worry for Manuel's safety. "You want to ruin your son's life, too?"

Escalante narrowed his gaze. "He's *my* son. He belongs with *me*."

Surprised that such an evil man would express such sentiment, Alessandro said, "You don't deserve him."

"He's *mine!*"

His tone conveyed volumes. "As an object of possession, not a child for you to love."

Escalante's mouth twisted. "We'll build a life together far from here. Father and son."

Alessandro gave a dry laugh. "You'll never be free. No matter where you go, they'll find you."

"Maybe, maybe not." Escalante rubbed his chin with his free hand. "What did Dahlia tell me?"

He seemed lost in thought for a second then his eyes lit up. "Ah, yes. *You* have a child."

Fear the size of a boulder lodged in Alessandro's throat. He'd been so careful to keep Mia's existence silent. "I don't know what you're talking about."

"I think you do." Escalante moved closer, his breath sour. "I think we can make a trade."

Wary, yet looking for an opportunity to escape, Alessandro asked, "What kind of trade?"

"I let you go, you lead Interpol, the FBI and whoever else away from me, while I retrieve my son. In exchange, I'll promise not to kill your child."

Alessandro's heart clutched with terror and rage. He kept his response in check. "There is no child," he stated, his voice flat.

"Yes, there is," a female voice countered.

Dahlia Sainsbury walked in through the tunnel, her vivid red pantsuit and tall heels looking woefully out of place in the earthen room. Her dark hair was pulled back in its customary roll and her heavily made-up eyes stared at Alessandro coldly. "You stole from me."

She came close and slapped him, stinging the already tender spots where Escalante had hit him. Alessandro gritted his teeth, not wanting to give either of them any satisfaction in his pain.

"You're easily duped," Alessandro ground out. "You let this amoeba turn you from your own brother."

Her eyes darkened. An expression akin to panic slid across her face.

Escalante grabbed her by the arm. "What is he talking about?"

Her red lips twisted into a seductive smile and she stroked her hand along his arm. "Nothing. He lies to distract us from his child."

Malice shone brightly in her gaze when she turned toward Alessandro. "Your cheeky little reporter friend told me about the child that you have hidden away. Didn't take much time at all to locate the brat. Money does talk."

Alessandro swallowed against the torment of impotent rage flooding him. He'd warned Colleen that her snooping would get someone hurt. He'd never dreamed it would be Mia. He'd been an idiot to allow his feelings for Colleen to impair his judgment.

In that moment, he realized the price his quest for

justice had cost him: the safety of his child. Regret sliced through his heart, wounding him as deeply as if Escalante had put a bullet through his chest.

After what seemed an interminably long period of time, during which Colleen searched the suite looking for a way to escape other than jumping from the balcony and praying she landed on the one below without breaking her neck, she finally settled on the couch with the Bible she'd found lying beside the bed in the master bedroom.

She'd wondered at first if the well-worn book belonged to Alessandro or Tomas, but the inscription in the front jacket warmed her heart. The leather-bound Bible belonged to Alessandro, given to him by his grandmother.

Restless and unable to focus, Colleen flipped through the pages, searching for…something to bring order to her chaotic emotions and anxious mind. She came to the Book of James and began to read from the beginning verse. The words touched her deeply, bringing the much-needed peace she craved.

Her heart knew that God loved her, that He loved Alessandro and Tomas. God's word said to ask in faith without doubting. She'd asked for protection for the Donato brothers. Closing her eyes, she held on to the promise that God would answer her request.

A sharp knock on the door broke the stillness of the room. She jumped up and ran to the door. Through the peephole she saw Lidia Vance. "Thank you, Lord," Colleen breathed out.

"Lidia! Lidia, it's me, Colleen. I'm trapped in here!" she yelled, hoping the woman on the other side would be able to hear her and let her out.

A second later the door clicked and opened. Lidia walked in, her plump frame clothed in dark colors that for a moment brought an ache to Colleen as she thought about the danger Alessandro and Tomas could be in. She threw her arms around Lidia's neck. "I'm so happy to see you."

Lidia patted her back. "Hey, now. I'm happy to see you, too. Where's that rascal nephew of mine?"

Colleen broke out of the embrace, her heart racing as she tried to explain what was happening. "We must phone Sam and Becca, let the police know what's going on. Do you have a phone? Alessandro did something to the phone here. It doesn't work."

Lidia nodded and pulled out a small cell phone from her purse. "That's why I came. I couldn't get through."

Colleen went in search of her purse but froze in shock as she listened to Lidia talking on the phone. Had she said Falcon? What was going on?

Colleen grabbed her purse and hurried over to Lidia as the older woman flipped her phone closed.

"Reinforcements are on the way," Lidia announced.

"Who's Falcon?" Colleen asked.

"That's classified."

"Alessandro said Falcon was their CIA contact. How do you know Falcon?" Colleen pressed.

Lidia's mouth formed a disapproving line. "I told that boy he was getting too involved with you, but did he listen? No. You must forget everything you've learned about Alessandro."

"I can't." Knowledge was power. Everything she'd found out about Alessandro helped solidify her feelings. "But right now there are more important things to think about."

She swept past Lidia. "Let's go. I'll need to show Sam and Becca how to get into the tunnel from inside the museum." Colleen headed for the elevator.

"Hold up, young lady. You're going home."

Biting back her frustration, Colleen pushed the button. "No. I'm going to go to the museum."

"Colleen, you'll only get in the way."

"Argh. You sound like Alessandro. Sam won't think I'm in the way." The elevator doors slid open and she started to walk over the threshold. Lidia's hand on her arm stopped her. The doors slid shut again and the elevator went on its way without her.

"Listen to me," Lidia said, her voice gravely quiet and commanding. "This is bigger than the local police, and not something that can appear in the *Sentinel*. Too many lives are at stake. If you care for Alessandro at all, you'll back off and let us do our jobs."

"Us? Lidia, do you work for Interpol as well?"

Lidia sighed. "No."

All the bits and pieces of conversation played themselves out in Colleen's head. "If not Interpol, then...you must be CIA."

"Colleen, please let it go."

Stabbing the elevator button again, Colleen said with complete conviction, "You're Falcon. Unbelievable. Does the mayor know? Of course he knows."

A thought jumped at her and the anticipation of a juicy story quickened in her gut. "Mayor Max Vance is a CIA operative as well, isn't he?"

One look at Lidia's frown confirmed Colleen's suspicion. "Wow. This is big."

"I'm getting too old for this," Lidia muttered. "Colleen, what are you going to do?"

The elevator doors opened and Colleen stepped in. "I'm going to help Alessandro and Tomas. Are you coming?"

Lidia chuckled and stepped in beside her. "I know why Alessandro likes you. You're as stubborn and as strong-willed as he is."

Colleen grinned and tucked Lidia's words away in her heart. She hoped that Alessandro more than liked her. *Fond* was the word he'd used. But could he love her? And could she—she swallowed back a nervous flutter—love him?

Could her faith be strong enough for both of them?

Only time would tell.

TWELVE

Seeing that Escalante had turned his attention to his drugs, Alessandro seized the opportunity to work at loosening the duct-tape restraints binding his hands and feet with the sharp edge of the band on his wristwatch.

He kept his movements miniscule so as not to draw notice. The band had been specially designed for such an occasion. Grateful to the clever minds who'd invented the device, he carefully sawed at the tape.

Men moved the crates filled with the cocaine that plagued the streets of Colorado Springs out of the cavern, undoubtedly to awaiting trucks. Alessandro's brother lay in a heap a few feet away, unconscious and bleeding.

With renewed vigor, born out of anguish and frustration, Alessandro pulled against the weakened fastening. He had to save his brother. He sent up a silent plea to God. *Could use some help here! I know I've shut You out, but Tomas hasn't. He needs You.*

Colleen's words came floating back to Alessandro. *He won't move in your life until you seek Him.*

Alessandro had stopped seeking the Lord years ago, even before Paola. Was that the emptiness he felt?

Tomas had tried to tell him he wasn't looking in the right places for fulfillment. Alessandro had not wanted to hear it. His life had become about the work. And then after Paola's death, his life became about seeking the justice that he felt God had denied.

Now, he couldn't ignore the truth in Colleen's words.

And he vowed to himself that he'd renew the faith he'd once held so dear. If he survived.

Raised voices drew his attention. Escalante and Dahlia were arguing. She stomped off, disappearing through the tunnel leading back toward the museum. The malicious expression on Escalante's face as he watched his cohort walk away didn't bode well.

When Escalante turned that malevolent stare on to Alessandro, Alessandro realized with a slight shudder he was looking into the dead, cold eyes of pure evil.

"So, have you thought about my offer? Your daughter in exchange for leading the imbecile police away from Colorado Springs?"

The bindings at Alessandro's wrist slackened, giving him hope. He fought to keep his struggle with the tape subtle so as not to alert Escalante. "Why do you want to stay here? Wouldn't Europe be more profitable?"

"Make no mistake, when all is said and done I'll be a rich man, but revenge is sweet and I want my share."

"Revenge on who?"

Escalante gave an arrogant smirk. "That's my business. Yours is whether I send someone to take out your child or you help me."

The man was beyond mad. His plan didn't even make sense. "So you'll let me go either way?"

Escalante barked a harsh laugh. "No, but you'll die not knowing if your child will be joining you in the grave."

"You're a sick man," Alessandro spat out and lunged forward in the chair.

The violent movement wrenched his arm, sending pain radiating through his shoulder into his head, but one wrist came free. To cover the surge of victory, he thrashed in the chair, making a big display of anger and frustration as he peeled the other wrist free from the tape.

Escalante's deep laugh grated on Alessandro's nerves and he couldn't wait to wrap his hands around the man's neck.

Sudden shouts and the reports of gunfire filled the chamber, abruptly cutting off Escalante's laughter.

"You're done for now, Escalante," Alessandro gloated, as he acquired the use of both hands. He bent forward to undo the tape at his ankles. From the corner of his eye he saw Escalante grab the gun that lay on the table and aim it in his direction. Heart pounding, Alessandro flung himself over sideways as the loud explosion of the shot deafened him in the small space.

Desperately working at freeing his ankles, Alessandro used the toppled chair seat as cover. "There's nowhere for you to go, Escalante! You're done for. Give it up."

"Ha! You think I don't have an escape planned?" Escalante's laughter faded away.

Alessandro released his ankles, crouched and peered over the chair in search of his quarry.

The man had disappeared.

Grinding his teeth in frustration, Alessandro rushed to his brother. Tomas had an erratic pulse. Some of the panic eased from Alessandro's shoulders. He gathered his brother into his arms. "Stay with me, Tomas. Mama will box my ears if you die."

The sound of running feet coming from seemingly all directions echoed down through the tunnels. Within moments, the chamber was awash with CIA, FBI and DEA agents. Alessandro demanded a radio and contacted Interpol headquarters, informing them of the danger to his daughter. They promised to protect her until he could arrive to be with her.

In the hubbub of getting Tomas secured with the authorities and taken to the hospital, and filling in the other agents on what had transpired, Alessandro caught a glimpse of a blond-haired vision. Colleen.

His heart did a double take, but he quickly forced his attention away. The woman had jeopardized his child's life with her investigating. He would never forgive her for that.

Focusing his mind on how Escalante had escaped, he searched the cavern walls and found a small latch concealed to look like a protruding rock. With a quick flick, a panel swung inward, revealing yet another tunnel. He rushed into the darkness, but this time thoughts of justice were crowded out by terror for his daughter's safety.

He had to find Escalante before the man fulfilled his threat to hurt Mia.

Colleen's heart stuttered and dropped as she watched Alessandro disappear into the dark tunnel. Alone.

Frantic worry propelled her forward. She stopped short at the opening. Everything inside her screamed to follow him, but what if she *did* get in the way?

What if she distracted him and Escalante seized the opportunity to hurt Alessandro?

In a panic, she grabbed one of the agents who'd met Lidia and her at the museum. "Alessandro needs backup. He went in there." She pointed to the gaping hole in the wall. "Hurry."

Without waiting for further explanation, the agent motioned for two other agents to accompany him and they disappeared after Alessandro. A bit of relief released the breath held in her lungs, but she wouldn't be at ease until she knew Alessandro was all right. Just the thought of him getting hurt or killed froze her heart. There was so much left unsettled between them. So much she wanted to say.

She saw Sam Vance and Becca Hilliard enter the chamber, and from the thunderous expression on Sam's face, Colleen surmised he was none too happy to be the last called to the scene. She started toward the two detectives. A hand on her arm stopped her.

"Everything you know, Colleen, is privileged information. Please, be responsible with it," Lidia said in a low voice.

Colleen winced with trepidation. "I can't promise anything. I have a story that needs to be told." A story that would put her at the top of the heap, garner her the recognition she'd being working so hard for. But she had no idea how to reconcile her need for the story with her feelings for Alessandro.

The disappointment in Lidia's eyes before she turned away tugged at Colleen's conscience.

"Aunt Lidia, Colleen? What are you two doing here?" Sam joined them, his puzzled, angry gaze raking over them.

Lidia hooked her arm through Sam's. "I'll explain everything."

She led him away, leaving Colleen feeling alone and in the way.

She understood what both Lidia and Alessandro wanted from her. Her silence.

But how could she ignore the story of the drug raid and the return of Escalante? This story could galvanize her career, maybe even create enough buzz to syndicate her writing.

First and foremost she was an investigative reporter. She had to stay true to her job.

She only hoped Alessandro would understand that.

Colleen hurried to the local hospital's waiting area, where the lady at the administration desk had said Tomas's family had gathered. The windowed area with its yellowing tile floor and hard, uncomfortable chairs was filled to overflowing with the Vance family.

Alessandro faced her as she approached, his expression hard and unreadable.

Her heart leapt into her throat and relief flooded her like a tidal wave. He was all right.

She touched his arm. "Is Tomas okay?"

Alessandro's eyes regarded her warily. "He's in surgery."

"Did you get Escalante? Dahlia?"

"No comment." He moved out of her reach.

Stung by his withdrawal, she bit her lip. He was angry, obviously. She thought she knew the reason. Lidia must have informed him that Colleen hadn't promised to keep all that had transpired confidential, but then again, she had a hard time reading him. That was one of the things that fascinated her about him.

She followed him to the window where he stared stonily out at the night sky. They were a few feet from the others, so she asked, "Do you want to tell me, off the record, what happened?"

"How do I know you'll keep your word not to print anything I say?"

Disappointed by his lack of trust, she countered, "I've never lied to you. I've never made a promise I couldn't keep."

He stared out the window. "No. You've made no promises, as far as I know."

She gritted her teeth. "You've only asked for one promise and I couldn't make it. That doesn't make me untrustworthy. I promise I won't use anything you tell me now in my story."

"What does it matter? Escalante escaped. So has Dahlia."

"I'm sorry. I know how much you wanted to capture him."

"Capture? I want him dead." Frustration echoed in his words. "When will justice prevail?"

She understood his feelings and wanted to soothe his ravaged soul. "Only God can deliver true justice. If you'd taken Escalante's life, then you'd have done something that only God should do. You can't keep trying to do God's work."

"I don't want to hear this." He took a step away.

Acknowledging to herself she was there for Alessandro and not her story, she followed. "You can't outrun God."

He glanced at her and scoffed. "You have no idea how much damage you've caused."

She drew back. "By bringing you backup?"

"It wasn't your place to provide my backup. You should have minded your own business, as I asked you to in the first place."

A spark of anger surged. "I saved your sorry hide and you treat me like this? You ungrateful man. If Lidia hadn't come to see why the phones weren't working, Tomas might be dead and so could…" Her voice broke as her words reminded her of the fear she'd felt for his safety. "You."

He let out a heavy breath. "I am grateful for that. But what I don't appreciate is you meddling in my private life and letting the world know about Mia."

She wrinkled her nose. "What are you talking about? I haven't written my story yet. No one knows about Mia."

He turned to face her fully, his eyebrows low and a furious tic in his jaw. "You meddled, no matter what kind of spin you put on it. Escalante now knows about my daughter because of you. And he's threatened her life."

Her stomach plummeted. She remembered asking Dahlia about the relationship with Alessandro, the calculating look in her eye when Colleen had mentioned the child. "I'm sorry. I didn't—"

"You didn't what? Mean to endanger my child? Mean to expose a little girl to the whims of a madman? You didn't think before snooping into something that was none of your business."

Her defenses rose. "Hey, that's not fair. I didn't know Dahlia was a criminal at the time and I certainly didn't know about Escalante. You didn't trust me enough to tell me why you wanted me to back off."

"Would it have made a difference?" he asked harshly.

She opened her mouth to respond, and then paused.

Searching her heart, she asked herself the same question.

Investigating, pushing for answers was an innate part of her makeup. She lived and breathed journalism. Since childhood she'd never accepted a simple answer or a "because I said so" from her parents and she certainly didn't accept such answers in adulthood. There was always a deeper meaning, a hidden motivation that needed to be brought to the light.

Was that why she'd pursued questioning Dahlia Sainsbury? Had she sensed the other woman's duplicity? Or had Colleen's need to push for answers on the relationship between Dahlia and Alessandro stemmed from some more personal reason?

She had to admit to herself that for the first time in a very long time she wanted to see where a relationship with a man would lead. She'd dogged Dahlia because Colleen had needed to know what obstacles lay in the way.

"In some ways, yes. It would have made a difference." She could see that now. "I wouldn't have let my emotions control my mouth."

He ran a hand through his dark hair, leaving grooved tracks. "You're not making sense."

"I wanted to know about the nature of the relationship between you and Dahlia."

"Why? Why must you know everything?"

She gritted her teeth. Time for a grain of truth.

If for no other reason than her own need for honesty. And a hope that maybe…maybe a relationship between them might work out. "I was jealous of her. You and I had…well, gotten along pretty good and Holly had told me about you saving her and Jake and I just didn't want to make a fool of myself by letting my attraction to you be known without finding out if you were involved with someone else."

He stared at her for a long time, his dark eyes unreadable. He shook his head, a grim set to his jaw. "This is my fault. I let my feelings for you cloud my judgment and my desire to protect you backfired."

She melted inside. He had feelings for her. What she'd been experiencing hadn't been one-sided. "You did protect me when Dahlia tried to poison me."

He closed his eyes for a second. When he lifted his lids, his dark eyes were flinty. "I didn't want you to become caught up in all this. I thought your snooping would get you hurt. I never considered your job would cause such problems…. I should have stayed far away from you."

A flash of hurt seared her to the quick. "Snooping? I'm not some busybody out to get the juicy gossip. I've done a lot of good with my investigations and my reports. I'm good at what I do. I deserve your respect, not your disapproval."

His gaze hardened and she shivered. "This time, your 'investigating' has put an innocent child in danger. *My* child. There's no way to undo what you've done. You tell me, how could God be pleased at that?" He spun away and left her standing there. Alone.

The conspicuous glances of the Vances brought a heated flush to her cheeks.

Guilt swamped her. She could only pray that God would cover her mistake and keep little Mia safe.

Colleen stared at the tall broad back of Alessandro and a fresh ache throbbed where his angry words had settled in her soul. He'd shut her out, effectively closing off any chance for a future together.

A gray-haired man wearing green scrubs and wire-rimmed glasses stepped into the room. The Vances moved around him and Colleen moved closer but stayed on the fringe of the semicircle. She wasn't one of them. She was an outsider, an interloper to the family.

"Surgery went well. He's in recovery. The bullet went through his shoulder. He lost a lot of blood so he'll be weak for a while, but he'll be fine."

"Praise the Lord," breathed Lidia.

"When can I see him?" asked Alessandro.

The doctor blinked at him, clearly taken aback by Alessandro and Tomas's striking resemblance. "Oh, you can come now."

Sam stopped Alessandro. "Hey, just to let you

know, cousin, you're obviously no longer a suspect in the mayor's shooting."

Alessandro's mouth quirked. *"Grazie."*

"Yeah, well, it would have been nice if you'd let me know what was going on."

Alessandro shrugged. "I'm afraid I operate on a need-to-know basis."

Colleen's heart bumped in her chest. He'd felt she needed to know how he felt. Why?

Sam nodded. "Now what?"

"After I see my brother's all right for myself, I return to Europe. I have unfinished business."

Colleen stifled the urge to ask if he were going after Escalante or to protect his child. Why didn't he tell his family of his little girl? It seemed so wrong to keep her a secret.

Sam frowned. "You can't leave town. You and Tomas are the only ones who know what Escalante looks like. Tomas won't be able to give us a description for a while. I need you to sit with a sketch artist."

"Don't have time. I'll do it in Europe and fax you a copy."

Sam grunted. "Fine. Just make it a priority."

"Will do." Alessandro started forward.

Colleen stepped into his path. She had one last shot at making things right between them. They deserved a chance. She needed to know why he'd told her of his feelings. "We're not done. I'll wait for you."

"Don't." A hard, implacable expression settled on his handsome features, warning her not to push. "Goodbye, Colleen."

Her heart cracked in her chest at the finality in his tone. Their relationship had died before it had even had a chance to be explored. The first man in her life to make her question how she defined herself was walking away.

She'd so been afraid of loving and losing that she'd never really allowed herself to feel. But now she felt all the pain and sorrow that losing could bring.

And she hadn't even told Alessandro how deep her feelings ran. She hadn't realized how deep those feelings ran until the moment it was too late.

Not knowing what to do now, Colleen looked around the room at all these people she knew and loved, but she felt so alone.

She hugged her arms to her chest and fought back tears. Lidia broke away from the others and put an arm around her. "Been quite the day."

Nodding, Colleen leaned into the older woman's embrace. "I'd like to go home now."

"Of course, dear." Lidia steered her over to Sam. "Can you arrange for Colleen to go home?"

"No problem, Aunt Lidia." He softened his voice

and snagged Colleen's hand. "I'll have Becca take you home, Colleen. Though I would like you to come to the station in the morning to wrap up the investigation on Neil O'Brien's murder. With Alessandro's testimony and Escalante's reappearance, I'm sure you'll be officially cleared of any wrongdoing."

"Gee, thanks," Colleen muttered, still a little ticked that Sam would have thought for even a second that she'd had anything to do with any murder. But logically she knew he was just doing his job.

As she'd been doing hers. And would continue to do.

Within a few minutes, Becca and Colleen were headed across town in Becca's sedan.

Colleen leaned her head against the cool window and thought of Alessandro. Would he face Escalante again? If so, who would survive?

The drama was getting to her. She wished they were ordinary people with ordinary lives. Then maybe…maybe she and Alessandro could have worked out.

She wondered how Becca did it, how she kept focused without needing a relationship.

"Do you ever wonder if it's worth it?" Colleen asked.

"Worth what?"

"Being married to your career. Putting the job

first. You and Sam didn't work out. Was it because of your careers?"

Becca glanced at her. "Partly. We do better as partners than as a couple."

"Do you think it's possible to have a successful career *and* be part of a couple?"

"Sam does it. He and Jessica are great together. She understands the job and helps Sam deal with the stress. And when they married, Sam became the family man he wanted to be with Amy, his step-daughter, and now the twins."

"You don't want a family? Because of the job?"

Becca shook her head. "No. I raised one family already when I took care of my siblings after our parents died. I have no desire to do it again. But Sam proves it's possible to be a good family man and a good police officer."

Colleen nodded, considering what Becca had said.

But Colleen's job had endangered Alessandro's child. How could she and Alessandro ever move past that?

Regret weighed heavily on her conscience. If only he'd trusted her enough to tell her what was going on.

But then again, she hadn't exactly done anything to earn that trust. No, she'd kept pushing for answers.

Becca pulled the sedan to the curb outside of Colleen's parents' home. The house was ablaze with lights. The door opened and Liza and Frank Montgomery rushed out, concern etched on their faces. Colleen's heart swelled with love for her parents. "Thanks, Becca," she said as she opened the door.

"Sure. Don't forget to come to the station tomorrow morning. It won't take long."

"Okay." Colleen closed the car door and hurried into her parents' embrace. Her heart squeezed tight. As much as she valued her parents' love, the arms she wished were holding her were probably already on their way to Europe.

Please, God, keep Alessandro safe. And ease the ache in my soul.

THIRTEEN

The next morning, Colleen awoke with a heavy heart. She'd dreamed of Alessandro, of his smile and tender concern. She'd dreamed he'd come back to her, declaring his love and taking her into his arms, making her feel special and safe.

But with the sunshine came reality. Alessandro was gone and she had to get on with her life without him.

Al Crane, her editor, would want her story ASAP. For the first time in her career she didn't look forward to putting to paper what she knew of the events that had transpired during the past few weeks.

She dragged herself out of bed, showered and dressed. After firing up her laptop, she sat staring at the blank screen. Her mind refused to think, to conjure up the words that usually flowed freely from her brain to her fingertips.

Coffee. She needed coffee.

Downstairs she encountered her mother sitting at the kitchen table, her Bible open and her study guide spread out before her.

"Morning, Mom."

Liza looked up and smiled, her green eyes lighting up with pleasure.

"Good morning, sweetheart." She opened her arms wide.

Colleen leaned into her mother's embrace and breathed in the faint scent of herbal shampoo in Liza's graying blond hair. "Where's Dad?"

"He's gone to see Max. With what you told us last night, your father figures he should offer his advice and support to the mayor."

Colleen made a noise of acknowledgement as she stepped out of the embrace. When she'd arrived home last night, her parents had grilled her like beef on the barbecue.

Frank Montgomery had ranted about the incompetence of the police for letting Escalante escape a second time, while Liza had tried to calm him down. Liza was always trying to keep Frank's blood pressure from rising. She had no intention of becoming a widow because of a heart attack just yet.

Colleen had shared with them Alessandro's true role in hunting down Escalante. She'd listened with wry amusement as her parents had claimed they knew all along he was a good boy. He was related to the Vances, after all. And the Vances and Mont-gomerys stuck together.

Not this Vance relative. He'd gone back to Europe.

Colleen had been wiped out emotionally by the time her head hit the pillow.

The strong smell of roasted coffee beans teased Colleen's senses, reminding her of why she'd come downstairs. She grabbed a white porcelain mug with a picture of a grinning calico cat on it from the rack of mugs hanging on the wall. She poured herself a full cup of steaming coffee and then sat down in the empty chair across from her mother.

Liza arched a brow. "You don't look as though you slept well."

"I didn't." Colleen knew there were dark circles under her eyes, but she'd rather ignore them.

"Why don't you go back to bed? I don't think anyone would fault you for needing to rest," Liza said.

Colleen shook her head. "Can't. I have a story to write."

"But you're stalling. I know you. You never sit down with me in the morning. You're always too busy with the next project. So why does this story have you looking so down? Escalante's return should make good fodder for the *Sentinel*."

Colleen sighed. "I know. And it will. This could be the story of a lifetime. It's just…I've uncovered some very sensitive information. I want to do the responsible thing."

"Which is?" Liza probed.

Colleen ran a hand through her tousled hair. "I'm so confused, Mom. I used to believe the public had a right to any and all information I could find on any given subject. But what if that information puts someone's life in jeopardy?"

"That *is* a dilemma. Only you can decide if what you know will make a difference for the greater good."

"The people of Colorado Springs need to know about Escalante's return and his escape."

A knowing look entered Liza's eyes. "But you're not struggling with Escalante, are you?"

Colleen pulled her bottom lip between her teeth. Were her feelings for Alessandro so transparent? "No."

"Alessandro?"

Apparently she was wearing her feelings on her sleeve. "Yes."

Liza reached across the table and took Colleen's hand. "Honey, I love you and I will always be proud of you no matter what you do. More than anything, I want you to be happy."

Colleen squeezed her mother's hand and fought back the sudden tears burning behind her eyes. "I love you, too, Mom."

"I know you do, dear." Liza gave her an indulgent

smile. "Love is a very complicated emotion. Yet it's also simple. That's why God's word says the greatest thing we can do in life is love others."

Colleen nodded, not sure where her mother was going with this conversation.

"Do you remember when you found that stray cat at the schoolyard when you were, what, ten?"

"Yes, ten." The cat had shown up at school and wouldn't leave her alone. It had waited outside the school doors until she appeared every day for a week. She'd finally decided to bring it home.

Her parents had not liked the idea of a stray animal in their house. Who knew what kind of diseases the cat carried? Plus the expense. Her parents had insisted she take it to the pound. She'd cried for three days.

"Do you remember what you did?" Liza asked.

Colleen grinned. "I went to the pound and bought the cat with the money I'd earned from cleaning the bathrooms and washing the cars."

"That's right. You loved that cat and weren't going to let anything stand in the way of your having it." Liza chuckled. "I still remember you carrying that scrawny bag of bones into the house with a huge triumphant smile as you announced that Pipsqueak wasn't a stray any longer. He was bought and paid for."

Colleen giggled. "Daddy about had a coronary right then."

"Yes, he did. But we all got used to him. And that cat loved you. I don't think I've ever seen an animal so devoted to a human before or since."

A nostalgic pang of sadness strummed through Colleen. Pipsqueak had lived a long life in cat years and had died peacefully in his sleep at the foot of Colleen's bed several years ago.

Liza dipped her head to capture Colleen's gaze. Colleen pushed away her sadness from the loss of her cat and concentrated on her mother.

"My point is, God brings love into our lives and we have a choice to make. We either give love back and fight for the health of that love or we let it go. But whatever choice we make, it is our choice." Liza withdrew her hand. "Now, off with you to write the story of a lifetime and then try to get some rest."

Pondering her mother's words, Colleen headed back upstairs and sat at her computer. For several long, agonizing moments she just sat. Then she forced herself to start, every word wrenched out, slicing through her.

It should be easy to write of Escalante's return and escape, but to do the story justice, she needed to tell it all. Her mind rebelled against revealing any of the events that's she'd witnessed that involved Alessandro, Tomas and Lidia Vance.

But the story had to be written. The world needed to know, and it was her job to inform them.

Only you can decide if what you know will make a difference for the greater good.

Doubts and questions swirled in her head. Would the public benefit from the information about Alessandro, Tomas and Lidia? Would the information change the world for the good? Or would it just sell more newspapers and in the process endanger their lives?

Her e-mail message light flashed, giving her an excuse to delay the inevitable. She clicked on the first message. Al, reaming her out for not reporting in and for not giving him a story.

She couldn't put her boss off much longer, so she picked up the phone and dialed the *Sentinel*. A knot twisted in her stomach while she held the phone away from her ear as Al yelled, demanding to know where her story was. Didn't she realize the enormity of Escalante's return?

"How did you know about that?" she asked, puzzled more by the fact that she wasn't upset that she'd been scooped than she was about who'd leaked the information.

"I have my sources. I want your story on my desk by noon. We'll headline it in the evening edition."

She should be jumping with joy to have a byline on the front page, but she couldn't even muster a little hop of satisfaction. "I'll do what I can."

Al sputtered. "I want the best story you've ever written on my desk by *noon*. You got that?"

"Yes, I got it. See you then." Colleen hung up and slumped in the chair.

The e-mail message light continued to blink, reminding her she had more messages. She opened the next one and sat up straight. This one came from her contact in Italy.

After some digging and some bribing, which she needed to be reimbursed for, thank you very much, she had an address of where Mia Donato resided in Germany. Colleen's heart sped up.

If she could get this information this easily then so could Escalante. Her mind raced in a dozen directions. She knew Alessandro would move his child, most likely to his villa in Italy, but would they ever be safe? What of Colorado Springs? Was the city safe from Escalante? Why had the madman come back in the first place?

She had to move, do something, or she'd go crazy speculating and worrying. Saving what little she'd written, she took her laptop and went to the police station. Sam and Becca were waiting for her. They both looked tired.

Becca's long ponytail was a little messy, as if she'd tried to run her fingers through her hair but had forgotten about the band holding it back. She wore the same navy pants and white blouse as she'd had on the day before.

Sam needed a shave and his gray slacks and dark polo shirt were also the ones he'd been wearing when Colleen had seen him at the hospital. Obviously both detectives had spent a sleepless night investigating Escalante's return.

Colleen took a seat at Sam's desk, much as she'd done many times before when she'd come as a reporter asking questions about a suspect.

Sam searched her face. "You okay?"

Colleen shrugged. Though her brain felt trapped in a tornado of confusion, her heart was numb. The last time she'd been at the station, Alessandro had shown up. He wouldn't be showing up this time.

"Thanks for coming in. I wanted to let you know officially you are no longer a suspect in Neil O'Brien's murder, and I hope we can continue on as if none of this had happened."

Her mouth quirked. Go back to life before Alessandro? She wasn't sure she wanted to, because he'd touched her in a way no one else ever had. She had no choice but to go on living. But was surviving each day without him really living?

"Yeah, sure," she said.

Becca handed her a large clear plastic bag with her mother's blue scarf folded inside. "Thought you might want this back."

Colleen stared at the scarf. Dark-red stains marred the fragile silk.

"Toss it," she said and turned away from the reminder of the violence that had touched her life.

And of the man who'd touched her heart.

"What can you tell us about Escalante?" Sam asked.

Colleen pursed her lips. "I probably can't tell you anything Alessandro hasn't already."

"Escalante survived the plane crash and had plastic surgery. Did you get a look at him?" Becca asked.

Colleen shook her head. "I never saw him. Only Alessandro did."

"He's gone back to Italy," Becca stated.

"Yes, he has," Colleen agreed glumly. She'd messed everything up with her probing and pressing.

"Do I detect some disappointment there?" Sam asked, his eyes alight with curiosity.

Colleen stood, not wanting to discuss Alessandro with Sam right now. Sam might be a good friend, but her feelings for Alessandro were too new, too confusing and too painful to share. "I've got a deadline I need to meet. May I go?"

Sam rose, his brow creased. "Sure. You know you can talk to us, Colleen. If you need anything, we're here for you."

She nodded, gave Becca a quick smile and walked out.

She drove to the *Sentinel,* took her laptop inside and went to her cubicle in the far corner. A withered fern sat sadly on top of the tall metal filing cabinet, its feathery branches drooping over a stack of folders that needed to be filed.

Above the desk a shelf held reference manuals and more file folders. Amid the clutter on the desk a monstrous Rolodex took up a good portion of the work area. Only one picture graced her cubicle. A family photo taken at Christmas a few years earlier.

She cleared away some hand-written notes pertaining to the fire at the hospital and laid her laptop down. She fired the computer up and then stared at what she'd written, formulating in her mind words yet to be typed in.

Words that would reveal Alessandro's position as an Interpol agent.

Without that bit of information, the story would lack the surefire burst of journalistic oomph that a cover story should have. She reread through what she had written with a heavy heart.

She closed her eyes, asking God for guidance. Memories assailed her. The tender look in Alessandro's eyes right before he kissed her. The feeling of rightness his embrace had evoked deep in her soul. The laughter and the camaraderie they'd shared over the last few weeks.

I'm fond of you, he'd said when they were out on

the balcony. *I let my feelings for you cloud my judgment,* he'd said in the hospital.

He might not want to face the fact that he cared for her, but she was certain he did. But could he still?

In her mind she saw the angry and near-desperate, fearful expression on his handsome face the last time she'd seen him. His words of justice and the need to protect his child played over in her mind. *Your "investigating" has put an innocent child in danger.*

She couldn't undo what had already been done. But she could prevent any further damage.

She knew it went against everything she'd been taught about good investigative journalism, but her feelings for Alessandro outweighed the public's need for knowledge.

Taking a course of action she'd never thought herself capable of, she pressed her finger on the delete key. The cursor moved rapidly over the letters, wiping them clean.

"What are you doing?" Al Crane's harsh exclamation momentarily paused Colleen's finger. With grim determination, she pressed harder on the delete button as if to make it go faster.

"Hey, we need that story! I've saved you space."

Keeping her finger on the key, she swirled in the chair to face her boss. "This story isn't one that needs to be published."

"Don't get a crisis of conscience now. There's no time." Al's bushy eyebrows furrowed over his stormy eyes.

At peace with her decision, Colleen grinned. "Not a crisis of conscience. I'm protecting someone I love."

The unexpected admission startled her. Yet saying what she felt in her heart lifted her spirit. A heady, liberating joy solidified her decision. She would do whatever it took to win Alessandro's heart.

"Love?" Al nearly shrieked. "What's love got to do with the news? You better have a story for me within the hour or you'll be demoted to garden parties and weddings."

Glancing at the screen, Colleen felt satisfaction at seeing her byline and the title of her story disappear. She closed down the computer and stood. "I've got to run."

Al sputtered. "You're leaving? And going where?"

A delightful giddiness filled her soul. "Italy." She moved past Al.

He stomped along with her. "What could possibly be in Italy that's more important than having a featured cover story?"

At the doors leading outside, she paused, and with what she was sure was a blinding smile said, "The man I love."

FOURTEEN

"Stay there, Papa. I'll get my dolly."

Alessandro watched his five-year-old daughter, Mia, run up the wide, ornate mahogany staircase of his villa. Her little spindly legs and long flowing dark curls were so endearing.

A lump formed in his throat and an ache tightened his chest. He'd been so focused on justice that he'd missed his little girl growing up. When had she learned to speak so well? The last time he'd seen her, she'd barely been able to string two words together.

His friends with whom she'd been living had done such a good job of caring for Mia. Would he be able to do the same?

The Heinens were a good-hearted, childless German couple employed often by Interpol to take in and protect witnesses. They'd agreed to have Mia come live with them, telling everyone she was a distant niece.

Alessandro had felt secure in knowing the couple would protect his daughter with their lives as well as love her.

Greta Heinen had fawned over Mia the moment she'd laid eyes on her. Alessandro would be forever grateful that Greta and Karl Heinen had kept Alessandro's existence alive in his child's heart.

With each visit to his daughter and her caretakers, Alessandro came away with a better knowledge of parenting and his desire to be with his daughter grew.

What had Colleen said to him? *What could be more important than your daughter? Your responsibility is to your child.*

Guilt squeezed in on him. He'd lost so much time with Mia. He hadn't been there for the important firsts of babyhood. Her first tooth, her first word. The day she took her first step.

As he waited for his little girl to return, he vowed he'd not miss any more of her childhood.

But what of Escalante? He was still at large.

Alessandro had made a vow over his dead wife's grave to bring justice to those responsible for her death. Justice to the man behind the drug cartel that had supplied his wife with the poison she'd used to kill herself.

Your wife chose to abuse her body with drugs. No one forced her.

Alessandro closed his eyes against the truth of Colleen's words. No one had spoon-fed Paola the drugs; she'd taken them of her own volition. But the scourge of cocaine and other drugs was the insidious way it lured the body into needing more and still more until the mind could no longer control the body's desperate hunger for the drug.

And the person responsible for perpetuating that need had to pay.

How could Alessandro ignore that? Especially now that Escalante knew about Mia.

Since that night a week ago when Escalante had escaped capture, Alessandro had lived on heightened alert, sure that at any moment the madman would appear like some evil specter to fulfill his threat to hurt Mia. The trip back to Europe had been torture, as he feared each minute that Escalante would reach Mia first.

Falcon, who unbelievably had turned out to be his Aunt Lidia, had kept him apprised of developments in Colorado Springs. The drug warehouse had been dismantled, many of Escalante's henchmen taken into custody. Sam and Becca were following new leads on Neil O'Brien's murder as well as other incidents they now believed involved Escalante. The dots were starting to connect.

Dahlia had not resurfaced, nor had Escalante.

Alessandro had sat with an Interpol sketch artist

and had sent along a rough drawing of the new Escalante to the Colorado Springs police. He'd also taken every precaution when he'd removed Mia from his friends' home and brought her to live in his villa in Fabriano. Armed guards walked the perimeter, security cameras and motion detectors covered the entrances and windows. Yet he still worried.

Mia ran back down the stairs and skidded to a halt in front of him. "See, Papa?" She held up a blond-haired doll with long dark lashes framing blue eyes.

His heart squeezed at the resemblance to a certain blue-eyed blonde who had worked her way through his defenses. He missed Colleen. Missed her tough-as-nails attitude and the gentle caring woman beneath.

He missed the way she gave as good as she got and made no apologies for it. He missed her smile and her sharp wit. He didn't want to miss her and would have to learn to live with the ache of not having her in his life.

"Isn't she beautiful, Papa?" Mia danced from foot to foot.

Tenderness and pride blossomed in his heart for his little girl. She'd adjusted to the move very well and had freely given him her love. "*Sì, bellissima.* As are you."

He bent to kiss her thin cheek. She giggled and twirled away, an active motion that seemed typical for a child of five, but that bore the traces of the legacy her mother's drug use had left her with. The doctors said it was attention-deficit/hyperactivity disorder, brought on by Paola's use of cocaine while carrying Mia. A condition little Mia would have to deal with for her whole life.

Anger surfaced, riding Alessandro with recriminations of guilt for not having protected Mia from the moment of her conception. It didn't matter that he hadn't known that Paola was carrying his child when she left. He should have done something to stop his wife's drug use.

Logically, he realized the futile thought for what it was, his own need to be in control. He hadn't been able to control Paola. She'd made her own choices, just as Colleen had reminded him.

"Come, Mia, it's time for supper," he called to the little dynamo now running circles in the parlor.

She raced past him to the dining table and climbed into the high-backed seat. With her legs swinging and her birdlike elbows resting on the large dark cherry table, she looked small and vulnerable.

A giant mass of parental anxiety contracted painfully in his chest. He'd do anything for his child, protect her with his life. They were family and he intended that they should live as one.

He went to the chair at the head of the table. Minutes ticked by without his staff's appearance with the meal. Odd. Mia chatted incessantly about her doll.

Alessandro made the appropriate responses, but his senses were telling him something was amiss.

"*Scusa*, Mia. I'll see what keeps Signora Catania," he said as he rose from the table.

He strode to the kitchen, expecting to see his housekeeper and cook, the plump Mrs. Catania, bustling about the state-of-the-art kitchen.

The room was empty.

The counters cluttered with the makings of a meal interrupted sent a shiver of apprehension down his spine. The back door was ajar. The alarms weren't set until late at night because too many people needed to come and go from the house.

Now, he realized the foolishness of that course of action. He'd left them vulnerable. He reached for the 9mm weapon holstered at his ankle.

He stalked outside to the patio garden. He waited a heartbeat, expecting a guard to appear, but none came.

He whirled around and ran back to the dining room. Mia was gone from her chair.

"Mia!" he bellowed. Fear raced through his veins.

He ran to the entryway and flung open the front door. On the stoop one of his guards lay unconscious. Quickly, Alessandro checked the man's pulse. Alive.

Alessandro's blooded pounded in his ears as terror gripped his heart.

"Mia!" he yelled out into the night. *Please, God, don't let anything happen to her.*

A noise drew him toward the parlor.

The room appeared unoccupied. The ceiling-to-floor curtain fluttered. Calming his breath, Alessandro approached the curtain from the side.

Grasping the gold fabric, he yanked the material aside as he aimed his weapon, his finger pressing on the trigger in anticipation of an attack.

Mia giggled. "You found me!" she singsonged.

A rush of relief staggered him. Lowering his weapon, he dropped to his knees.

"Thank You, Lord above," he said aloud and drew her to him. "Sweeting, you must not scare Papa like that. Why did you leave the table?"

She stared up at him with wide brown eyes. "You left me alone. I thought we were playing hide and seek." Her lip pushed out. "You didn't count."

Taking deep breaths, he pushed to his feet with Mia in his arms. "Come, sweeting, we will play hide and seek for real."

He hurried over to the stairs, careful to avert her face from the sight of the guard lying in the open doorway.

"Hide your eyes, sweeting. Count to twenty," he said as he set her on the stair.

Burying her head on her folded arms, she complied.

Alessandro moved to the door and dragged the unconscious guard inside to the parlor. He shut and locked the door before returning to Mia. He scooped her up into his arms.

"Papa! I'm not done counting," she squealed.

"That's all right, *bella*," he said as he carried her to his office. Behind a false wall, he had a hidden room that he used for Interpol business. Every instinct in him screamed to secure her in the room and then go looking for the bad guys.

Your responsibility is to your child. Not to some job.

He would stay with Mia.

Once they were safely inside the square windowless room, he contacted headquarters using a special line he'd had installed that didn't connect to the main phone lines of the house. His superiors at Interpol assured him they'd send backup.

He checked the camera monitors. Nothing moved around the perimeter of the house. He could only pray the other guards and Signora Catania had fared as well as the guard he'd found at the entry door.

He sat on the brown leather couch with Mia on his lap. "We must be very quiet so we aren't found."

Wide-eyed, Mia nodded and snuggled into the crook of his arm. "Who's looking for us, Papa?"

"Bad people, sweeting."

She frowned.

"No worries, sweeting. I'll protect you." He kissed her forehead and she relaxed with a sigh.

This was what he'd been afraid of. That his life as an Interpol agent would endanger his child. That was why he'd kept her existence a secret. A secret exposed by Colleen's investigating.

But could he really place all the blame at Colleen's feet? If he'd trusted her with the knowledge of who he was and what he was after from the beginning, perhaps the situation would have turned out differently.

He rocked Mia and softly sang a song he remembered from childhood. She fell asleep with her head on his shoulder. He hugged her close, loving the feel of her in his arms. His heart swelled with love. And time ticked by.

A movement on the monitor showing the front of the villa froze his veins. It couldn't be!

Moving as swiftly as possible, he gently laid Mia on the soft leather cushion. She murmured a sleepy protest, then snuggled into the corner. Her breathing evened out.

Alessandro picked up the 9mm from where he'd laid it on the desktop. He slowly opened the panel and secured it closed behind him. Then he opened the outer office door, made sure the hall was empty, then stepped out and closed the door behind him.

"Hellooo," a female voice called out.

His heart rate jackknifed at the familiar American lilt.

Colleen.

He rushed down the stairs, his only thought to secure her safety before Escalante expanded his need for revenge to include her. She stood at the bottom of the stairs like a breath of fresh air in white capris and a blue shirt the exact color of her eyes, her blond hair loose about her shoulders.

She turned as he stormed down the stairs, her smile hitting him square between the eyes and forcing his lungs to contract.

He reached her side, grabbed her by the arm and pulled her up the stairs behind him. "You shouldn't be here," he growled.

Had she come for him or her story? He didn't dare analyze the question for fear of the answer. For fear of what he hoped she'd say.

"Well, hello to you, too." She yanked her arm from his grasp and halted. "What are you doing?"

Panic made his voice harsh. "We don't have time for this. Escalante's men are here."

Her dark blond eyebrows drew together. "Are you sure Escalante's here? Everything seems very peaceful. I walked in without any problems."

"My security team is missing. So is my housekeeper. What else am I to think?"

"They got better job offers?"

He ground his back teeth. "No. My staff wouldn't desert me. Only Escalante could have done this."

"Maybe some other villain you've ticked off lured your staff away. In your line of work, I'm sure there are more like Escalante popping up every day."

Irritated by the thought she'd planted and its validity, he moved up the steps. "Come, we must get to safety."

She nodded and followed him to the office. He wasn't ready to show her into the inner room where Mia slept. Yet. He didn't want Mia exposed to the press, if indeed Colleen was here in such a capacity. He wouldn't let his mind wander to any other conclusion.

"How did you get here?" he asked.

She cocked her head. "I swam across the ocean and hiked over the mountains."

He blinked and fought a smile. "I mean, how did you find my home?"

"Ahh." Her face scrunched up in a way that he found adorable. "Well, that was tricky. I've spent the better part of the day asking around town about you. A nice older man pointed me in the right direction. I drove my rented car here, though I must say you are tucked back a ways and I was sure I'd missed the house. But here I am."

"Here you are."

"And if I found you so easily, then Escalante probably could as well."

Of course what she said was true, but considering he was more than sure that Escalante had already found him he only nodded. Not sure how to feel or what to think about her sudden appearance back into his life, he just stared at her, soaking up the sight and soft scent of her.

He ached to take her into his arms, to hold her again. But so much lay between them.

She had a story to tell that would reveal his true identity and ruin his effectiveness as an Interpol agent. Not to mention he had a daughter to care for, to protect from exposure to the media.

And first and foremost Colleen would always be a reporter. He had to accept that. And accept that she could not be a part of their lives.

Something in his expression must have betrayed his thoughts, because she backed up, her hand closing around the door knob. An uncertain light entered her eyes. "This probably was a mistake. I see that. I should leave."

Before he could say anything she fled the room.

He rushed after her, his need to protect her overcoming his distress at seeing her. He caught her halfway down the stairs. "No, *bella*. You must wait."

The sound of heavy footfalls echoed through the ten-foot-high entryway. Alessandro pushed Colleen behind him as he crouched, his weapon drawn. Three armed flack-vested men filed in from the kitchen as two more men burst through the front door.

Recognizing fellow Interpol agents, Alessandro sagged with relief and slowly stood.

The man in front held up his fist as a signal to halt. "Mr. Donato. The perimeter is clear. The guards and your housekeeper were found alive and in fair shape in the pool house. None could identify their attackers."

Relief that his staff hadn't met a horrible end because of his job filled him. "Thank you. Please secure the premises."

"Bueno." The men melted back, disappearing into the night, and Alessandro felt a moment's peace to know Interpol agents were now protecting his child.

And Colleen.

She'd become important to him. More than he'd ever intended.

He turned to the woman leaning against the wall. *"Bella,* you are all right?"

"Oh, sure." She offered him a wry smile. "Life with you is one roller-coaster ride after another."

He scowled at her words and stated flatly, "We have no life together."

Her mouth quirked at one corner. "Well, now. That's what I came to see you about."

His stomach did a loop. He hated the hope stirring

inside his chest. He had no intention of letting her into his heart. "I do not understand. Your life is in America. You have family, a job. I'm…what I am. Our lives cannot mesh."

The blue in her eyes darkened with determination, chasing away the earlier uncertainty. "I know you blame me for endangering your daughter. You're right. I should have been more discreet. I've come to ask for your forgiveness."

Tenderness welled in his chest, but he fought against it. He'd made mistakes. They both had. But not even forgiveness could meld their lives. His life was too dangerous and too uncertain. As she'd pointed out, there would always be an Escalante lurking out there. He saw that now.

He would find another secure place for Mia, and this time he would be more careful in hiding her. Hiding a woman as independent and headstrong as Colleen would be impossible. "You have my forgiveness. Now you must leave."

The stunned expression in her eyes made him feel as if he'd slapped her. "Just like that?"

"Just like that," he repeated grimly, hating the anguish in her eyes. He didn't want to hurt her, had never meant for this thing between them to come to a point where she would look at him with such heartache.

"No." She lifted her chin in defiance. Her tenacity

was a palpable thing. "I'm not leaving. Not yet. We have unfinished business, buddy boy."

His admiration for her threatened to knock him flat. There was no doubt in his mind she meant what she said.

He wanted to take her in his arms and kiss her mouth until her lips softened and her breath came fast. But he held still, knowing that physical attraction did not equal a lifetime commitment.

Colleen was a lifetime kind of lady. And he refused to look too closely at the emotions growing in his chest.

"Papa?" Mia's groggy voice drew his attention. She stood on the landing, her little body swaying with residual sleep.

Heart in his throat, he vaulted past Colleen and caught Mia before she stumbled down the stairs. He held her close, sure she could feel his pounding heart. Clever little minx to figure out how to open the panel in his office. He would have to be careful not to underestimate her again.

"Who's that, Papa?" she asked in Italian, pointing to Colleen.

"A friend," he responded in English, hoping at least that was true.

Colleen joined them on the top stair. "Hi, little one. You must be Mia. I've wondered so much about you."

"Do you like dollies?" Mia asked, switching easily to English.

Colleen's smile invaded his senses. "I sure do."

Mia wiggled until Alessandro put her down. As soon as her feet touched the landing, she grabbed Colleen's hand and tugged. "I have many dolls. Come see."

Colleen stepped past him, her expression curious and gentle. Their gazes held. His gut clenched at having her so close and with his child. As if they were a family unit. *Stupido.*

Mia and Colleen disappeared into Mia's room. He sank to the step and put his head into his hands. *I don't understand, Lord. Why has she come here? To finish her story?*

A deep pain sliced through him. He didn't want her job to be the reason she was here, yet he couldn't hope that she was here for him. He couldn't envision a future with Colleen. Not with the way things stood. He'd have to go deep undercover now that his true identity had been revealed. Or at least, he would have to when she finished her story.

He rose, weary determination settling in. He would retrieve his daughter and tell Colleen to leave. That was the only course of action to take. His future belonged to Mia. He must think about what was best for her.

Pausing in the doorway of Mia's bedroom, the fight drained out of him. Colleen and Mia were curled up on Mia's pink flowered four-poster bed, surrounded by dolls and stuffed animals. The quiet chatter of his daughter and the occasional soft question from Colleen tore at his heart.

This was what Mia needed.

A mother who'd spend time with her, who would love her.

Colleen glanced up and smiled, a soft affectionate smile that made his knees tremble and his heart twist. He could no longer deny to himself that he'd fallen in love with Colleen Montgomery, investigative reporter extraordinaire.

Her innate kindness shone through her driven nature. She was a woman who was loyal and strong, who would love with her whole heart.

But the knowledge only saddened him. Loving her didn't change anything. He would never be more than a story to her.

Mia let out a big, noisy yawn. He strode forward and with Colleen by his side, they tucked Mia into bed. His heart ached at the domesticity of the scene. If only it could be real.

Colleen kissed the child's forehead before turning toward the door.

"Prayers, Papa?"

"*Sì.*" He knelt beside her bed and quietly thanked God for their safety and asked for a good night's sleep for Mia.

"And God, thank You for Colleen coming to visit. Amen," Mia added.

Pride and love for his daughter brought tears to the corners of his eyes. He kissed her good-night. He wasn't surprised to find Colleen standing in the doorway, her gaze misty.

He motioned for her to precede him down the stairs. He led her into the now-empty front parlor. "Colleen, you—"

She held up a hand. "No. Let me say what I came thousands of miles to say."

He nodded. She bit her lip as uncertainty once again crossed her features. His heart sped up. Would she ask for an interview? He couldn't grant her one. His breath stopped in the vicinity of his heart.

She swallowed. "I love you, Alessandro," she whispered.

His breath exhaled in a rush. He raised his eyebrows as her words sank in, stirring his soul with unfamiliar elation. A smile tugged at the corners of his mouth. That was his Colleen. No preambles. Blunt and to the point. Exactly the kind of woman he needed in his life.

She looked so vulnerable standing there with her heart shining in her eyes.

"Okay, you don't have to respond right away," she said. "I'm sure I've taken you by surprise. It took me by surprise. I never thought I'd fall in love, let alone hop on a plane and fly across the ocean to chase down a man who apparently doesn't feel the same way.

"But there you have it. I do. You're a good man. Kind, gentle, yet strong in so many ways. You live your convictions. And you are so good with your daughter. If I didn't already know I loved you, I'd have fallen in love with you for sure just now watching you pray with Mia."

Her words broke through the wall he'd shuttered his own feelings behind. He wasn't afraid to let the love and tenderness exploding in his heart overflow to fill every corner of his being.

She took a breath to continue, but he pulled her to him. She gave a surprised squeak before looping her arms around his neck.

"I can't go back once the world knows I'm an Interpol agent," he said, wanting to be sure she understood the way his life would have to be.

She cocked her head. "If anyone knows, they didn't hear it from me."

Bewilderment siphoned the blood from his head. For a moment the world tilted. He couldn't have heard her correctly. "What?"

Her earnest blue eyes gazed up at him. "I didn't turn in my story. You were right. Some things need to be strictly confidential. Though I'm sure Lidia informed your cousins."

Overwhelmed by her sacrifice, he stared. "I don't know what to say."

In a soft voice full of hope, she said, "Say you love me, too, and that you'll let me into your heart."

Risking his life was easier than risking his heart, but he couldn't imagine living without her. "But what of your career? It's your life."

Her beautiful mouth curve into a wry smile. "You know, they say truth is stranger than fiction. But fiction can sure mirror truth. I've decided to try writing fiction. Maybe suspense. Crime novels. I can do that from anywhere."

Humbled and touched to his soul by her admission and her willingness to find a new path, he touched his nose to hers. "You are an amazing woman, *bella*."

She sighed. "I love when you call me that."

"And I love you." He captured her mouth and breathed in her "Oh." Several moments later, he lifted his head. "*Bella,* life with me would always hold danger. I can't ask you knowingly to take that on."

"You don't have to ask. I'm offering. And I know it won't be easy. I'll worry. I'll probably get in your way sometimes trying to protect you and Mia. But I know what I want. I know what's important. And with God on our side, how can we lose?"

Her words convinced his soul. "I have to ask God for forgiveness. I've been operating on the need for vengeance and calling it justice. A wise lady told me that only God can deliver true justice. I wasn't ready to hear that before, but I am now. I'm ready to live that truth. I now know what's important, as well."

Colleen pressed her cheek to his chest and hugged him fiercely.

Floodgates of love opened, filling him to overflowing. He lifted her chin with the crook of his finger until their gazes met. "Will you do me the honor of marrying me and becoming a mother to Mia?"

"Only if you'll kiss me again," she teased and pulled him closer until their lips met.

A little girl's giggle came from the doorway. Colleen murmured against his lips, "Our daughter's watching."

A soothing peace filled Alessandro's soul as he and Colleen turned and opened their arms to Mia.

"Now we can be a real family," Mia declared with a huge grin as she ran to their embrace.

The three-way hug dissolved into laughter and tickles as the Donato family began their new life together.

EPILOGUE

Several weeks later, in a small, rustic cabin hidden in the woods outside Colorado Springs, Baltasar Escalante gripped the society page of the *Sentinel* with clenched fists. The article and accompanying photo stirred hatred and rage in his soul like molten lava waiting for the precise moment to explode.

The article announced the impending nuptials between Alessandro Donato, nephew of Mayor Maxwell Vance, and Colleen Montgomery, daughter of former mayor Frank Montgomery. The event would take place the following month and the couple, along with Alessandro's daughter, would be returning to live in Italy. The photo showed the two clans posing for the camera with smiles of joy on their faces.

Escalante growled low in his throat. He couldn't wait to wipe those grins off their faces. He might have been thwarted in Italy by Interpol agents, but he wouldn't allow that to happen again. They would pay. All of them. Time was growing short. But now he knew when and how to strike down the Vances and Montgomerys. He'd get them in their hearts. He'd make it very personal.

He laughed, a rusty sound that echoed in the silence of the cabin.

But first he had one little detail to see to.

Dahlia.

He should have guessed she was Alistair Barclay's half sister. No one played him for a fool and got away with it. Her double cross would be the end of her.

He crunched up the newspaper and threw it into the brick fireplace. The flames attacked the wad with gusto until nothing but ash remained.

The hypnotic dance of the blue, yellow and orange fire eased his tension and solidified his plans. He couldn't wait to attack his enemies with the same enjoyment as the flames. And when he was done… when he triumphed, there'd be nothing left but ash.

* * * * *

Dear Reader,

I hope you enjoyed book five of the FAITH AT THE CROSSROADS continuity series, I had fun writing the story of how Colleen and Alessandro worked together to find love and faith amid murder, mystery and mayhem.

I want to thank my sister Love Inspired Suspense ladies, Lois, Val, Sharon, Marta and Margaret. You all are an inspiration and a wonderful blessing to my life.

I have to say thank you to my family for your support and to Leah and Lisa for cheering me on.

The verse I chose for this story's theme is such a basic concept to faith. If we draw close to God, He promises to draw close to us. It's a reciprocal relationship that takes action on our part because God gives us free will to choose to reach out to Him. I hope that you will reach out to the One who loves you beyond all measure.

May God bless you all your days,

QUESTIONS FOR DISCUSSION

1. What made you want to read this book? Did you read the previous books in the continuity series? Did this book live up to your expectations?

2. Did you think Colleen and Alessandro were believable characters? What did you like about each one? What did you dislike? Did the characters grow through the story? Did the romance build believably?

3. Were the secondary characters essential to the plot? Were the villains realistic?

4. Was the setting clear and appealing? Could you "see" where the story took place?

5. Alessandro confused vengeance with justice. Do you ever seek vengeance and call it justice? Can we ever have justice? Is there anything constructive about vengeance? Who can deliver true justice?

6. Did Colleen's sacrifice at the end seem reasonable? Would you have made the same choice? Have you ever had to make a choice to put someone else's needs above your own? How did that make you feel?

7. Alessandro's late wife had a drug problem, and he tried unsuccessfully to break her addiction. Have you struggled or do you know someone who struggles with addictions? What steps can be taken to help someone become free from addiction? Do you believe a person must want to be free of their addiction before they can be set free?

8. Did the end pique your interest to read the next book in the series? If so, why? Or why not?

9. Did the author's use of language/writing style make this an enjoyable read? Would you read more from this author?

10. What will be your most vivid memories of this book? What lessons about life, love and faith did you learn from this story?

Violence against the Vance and Montgomery families has been escalating for months. And when the final confrontation with their old enemy comes at last, carpenter Quinn Montgomery and Colorado Springs police detective Becca Hilliard are in the middle of it all in Margaret Daley's *HEARTS ON THE LINE*....

And now turn the page for a sneak preview of *HEARTS ON THE LINE*, the last installment of FAITH AT THE CROSSROADS.

On sale in June 2006 from Steeple Hill Books.

"What brings you by?" Quinn handed his younger brother a mug full of hot, strong coffee, then filled a cup for himself.

"Heard about the jumper and came running. Couldn't see you going through this without me, especially with the trouble the family and the construction company have had lately. At first I thought it was connected to that."

"Nope. David James just lost it. His supervisor called him on being late for work. That sent the man over the edge. He flew at Collins, hit him a few times, then escaped up to the roof, where he threatened to jump."

"Is Collins okay?" Brendan asked.

"Yeah, just a cut lip and probably a black eye." Quinn lifted his mug to take a sip and noticed his hand shaking. He placed the mug on his desk before he spilled his coffee. "How does she do it?"

"How does who do what?"

"Becca. Negotiating." Quinn clasped his hands together to still their trembling, recognizing the reaction as delayed shock. When he had thought David would jump, all he could think of was the man's two little girls without their father. *Thank You, God, for delivering David safely down. And thank You for sending Becca to help.*

"Ah, now it's just Becca."

"Stop right there, little brother. After going through something like what happened on that rooftop together, it seems kind of ridiculous to call the woman Ms. Hilliard."

Brendon lounged against the file cabinet. "She has her own methods of distressing. We all do."

Quinn knew his brother was referring to people working in law enforcement. He'd been engaged to a woman who had been on the police force until— again his heart twisted with the remembrance of that day Maggie had died. So much for not going down memory lane.

"You're the boss. Give yourself the rest of the day off. I think you deserve it."

"So I can go over what happened on the rooftop until I go screaming down the street? No, thank you. I think I'll stay and work." Which was one of his ways of dealing with stress. Finally Quinn thought his hand was steady enough to pick up the mug and take a long drink of his much-needed coffee. "How's Chloe? Have you two set a date yet?"

Brendan chuckled. "I get the picture. No more talking about you. Chloe and I are negotiating when. Also, I've been helping Kyle with baseball, and her little girl is adorable. Definitely Chloe's the one."

"I'm glad, since you two are already engaged."

"How about you? Seeing anyone?"

"Don't have the time. The fire set me back some. Having to rebuild the shop and barn as well as do all the projects we're committed to has taken a lot of my extra time."

"I thought you finished the shop and barn a couple of weeks ago?"

"Yes, but…" Quinn let his sentence trail off into the silence. He and his brother knew the real reason he hadn't dated. Since Maggie's death three years ago, except for the few times Brendan had tried to fix him up, he hadn't gone out with anyone. Instead, he had thrown himself into his work and his carpentry.

"She would have wanted you to move on, Quinn."

"I know. I am. Colleen has a friend at the paper she wants to introduce me to. I'm thinking about taking her up on her offer once she returns from Italy for her wedding."

The second Quinn said that, however, an image of Becca up on the rooftop, totally focused on David, calm and in control, popped into his mind. *There's something about Becca Hilliard that—no, don't go there. Her job is as dangerous as Maggie's was, and Maggie's job killed her.*

Love Inspired

presents

a special Steeple Hill Café collection of books featuring fun, endearing heroines who experience the ups and downs of love and faith.

Steeple Hill Café™

May 2006
BE MY NEAT-HEART
BY JUDY BAER

June 2006
BLISSFULLY YOURS
BY DIANN WALKER

July 2006
ANY MAN OF MINE
BY CAROLYNE AARSEN

August 2006
MY SO-CALLED LOVE LIFE
BY ALLIE PLEITER

Look for these titles
wherever you buy your Love Inspired books.

REQUEST YOUR FREE BOOKS!

2 FREE INSPIRATIONAL NOVELS
PLUS A
FREE
MYSTERY GIFT

LoveInspired®

YES! Please send me 2 FREE Love Inspired® novels and my FREE mystery gift. After receiving them, if I don't wish to receive any more books, I can return the shipping statement marked "cancel." If I don't cancel, I will receive 4 brand-new novels every month and be billed just $3.99 per book in the U.S., or $4.74 per book in Canada, plus 25¢ shipping and handling per book and applicable taxes, if any*. That's a savings of over 20% off the cover price! I understand that accepting the 2 free books and gift places me under no obligation to buy anything. I can always return a shipment and cancel at any time. Even if I never buy another book from Steeple Hill, the two free books and gift are mine to keep forever.

113 IDN D74R 313 IDN D743

Name _____ (PLEASE PRINT)

Address _____ Apt. _____

City _____ State/Prov. _____ Zip/Postal Code _____

Signature (if under 18, a parent or guardian must sign)

Order online at www.LoveInspiredBooks.com

Or mail to Steeple Hill Reader Service™:

IN U.S.A.	IN CANADA
3010 Walden Ave.	P.O. Box 609
P.O. Box 1867	Fort Erie, Ontario
Buffalo, NY 14240-1867	L2A 5X3

Not valid to current Love Inspired subscribers.

Want to try two free books from another series?
Call 1-800-873-8635 or visit www.morefreebooks.com

* Terms and prices subject to change without notice. NY residents add applicable sales tax. Canadian residents will be charged applicable provincial taxes and GST. This offer is limited to one order per household. All orders subject to approval. Credit or debit balances in a customer's account(s) may be offset by any other outstanding balance owed by or to the customer.

LIREG05